Acclaim for *Berlin Garden of Erotic Delights*

"The publication of the 1920 *Berlin Garden of Erotic Delights*—five short fictions by Granand in its first English translation—is one of the most important discoveries of lost queer literature in decades. This panorama, filled with vivid details, of Weimar Republic's gay subculture is an amazing act of recovery. But the real revelation here is Granand's prose: poetic and precise, quirky and beautiful it captures perfectly jazz age tensions, excitement and sexuality as much as Scott Fitzgerald or Dorothy Parker. We have waited over a century for an English publication of *Berlin Garden of Erotic Delights* and it has been well worth the wait."
—Michael Bronski, author of *A Queer History of the United States* and Professor of the Practice in Activism and Media Studies of Women, Gender and Sexuality, Harvard University

"Granand's *Berlin Garden of Erotic Delights* is essential to understanding that gay life was not always subjugated, but that gay men in the 1920s enjoyed life and flourished. This book is a landmark achievement in reminding us that stories are crucial markers of human experience."
—Professor Joseph H. Hancock, II, Drexel University

"Michael Gillespie's translation of *Berlin Garden of Erotic Delights* returns to English-speaking consciousness an incredible slice of queer European life in the 1920s. Although clearly of their period, these stories reveal a vibrant queer world that will strike modern readers as immediately recognizable. Banned, suppressed, and long-forgotten, these stories deserve a place on any queer history reading list."
—Hugh Ryan, author of *When Brooklyn Was Queer*

BERLIN
GARDEN
OF
EROTIC
DELIGHTS

First Warbler Press Edition 2022

First published in 1920 by Almanach-Verlag, Berlin

Translation, Introduction, and Biographical Timeline © Michael Gillespie

Bal homosexuel au "Magic City" by George Brassaï, circa 1931.
© Estate Brassaï-RMN-Grand Palais

www.warblerpress.com

ISBN 978-1-9572-4024-4 (paperback)

ISBN 978-1-957240-25-1 (e-book)

BERLIN GARDEN OF EROTIC DELIGHTS

granand

TRANSLATED AND INTRODUCED BY MICHAEL GILLESPIE

AFTERWORD BY MANFRED HERZER

CONTENTS

INTRODUCTION
by Michael Gillespie

MY OBSESSION WITH GRANAND AND HIS FIVE SHORT STORIES on the theme of male same-sex desire began in the mid-1990s. I'd visited the Schwules Museum [Queer Museum] in Berlin, a grassroots effort that preserves and interprets the history of LGBTQ+ people, and believe that's where I purchased the 1993 reprint of Granand's 1920 publication, by Verlag Rosa Winkel... Or maybe it was at A Different Light bookstore (now defunct, of course, like so many independent bookstores) on Hudson Street in New York, near where I lived, and which would frequently offer the odd outlier on its shelves. My now husband, Marvin, remembers me standing in one of its aisles leaning against the shelves engrossed in reading the Granand text and looking up and telling him, "I need to buy this."...But I have no such memory. Whatever the case, this magical little collection came into my life and commanded my attention at a moment when I was looking to rekindle my engagement with German literature and with literary translation, which I'd set aside as I pursued nonacademic employment.

I've had an enduring interest, starting from the time of my graduate studies in comparative literature, in literary translation and in how texts mutate as they migrate from their domestic setting to a foreign one. This, combined with a concern for how gay lives are represented in culture, led me to look more carefully at this small gem I'd stumbled upon serendipitously. My discovery also coincided with a heady moment in queer theory that challenged traditional notions of gender and identity, and with the evolving nature of the AIDS epidemic, which was still very much a specter haunting gay life, contributing in New York City to a solemn, somber mood. And in the year 1993, my mom died on a frigid December morning in Minnesota. What Granand's stories could have to say to a young man faced with these realities at that particular point in time started to unfold for me as I began translating them.

I soon realized what lay before me in Granand's all-but-forgotten work was a collection of narratives whose frank depiction of gay lives and sensibilities celebrates the panorama of humanity and takes their erotic desires simply for granted. As I explain below, this is somewhat unusual even for the Weimar period, known today for artistic license resulting from the post-war government's bold yet short-lived decision to end all censorship, in 1919. The author's purpose is to portray a variety of characters in specific situations to offer what he himself, in a short note about the collection included in the original publication, called a "slice of life," carefully not specifying that his stories intended to capture a specifically *gay* slice of life, whether to avoid the censors, who nonetheless prohibited the book and pulped its first edition, or simply to underscore the ordinary, common, "garden variety" nature of their desires.

Granand writes about what he knows, the details of gay life, in a form with which he's familiar from his background in theater. Indeed, the stories read like short plays. The collection explores the characters' emotions, fantasies, and relationships, and does so with irony and wit, while the characters themselves become transformed through their experiences, allowing them to transcend their settings and imbuing them with interiority. The stories do not all end up well—how much in life does?—but for a short collection, Granand manages to portray a surprising range of characters: an unapologetically stylish aesthete who slyly gets the better of a rough-hewn burglar; a Swiss student of art history and a traveling American businessman whose chance meeting in a train compartment leads them to a one-night stand; two clubgoers, the main characters of a rom-com that also offers a glimpse into contemporary gay life in Berlin; a trio of cadets whose lives intertwine within the rigid confines of a military school, whose strictures I know all too well, having attended a similar institution—in my case, a Catholic military school for boys in St. Paul, Minnesota; and a character reminiscent of Gustav von Aschenbach, the doomed protagonist of Thomas Mann's 1913 novella *Death in Venice*, to which Granand cleverly alludes a few times. There is heartbreak and betrayal in Granand's stories, but also the thrill of discovering that one's passion is matched by another, the pleasures of dancing, celebrating, and flirting in public, the touch of a hand and the texture of skin, the peculiar happiness of falling in love. But even when Granand's stories take a melodramatic turn, which a writer like Mann would probably have disdained, they nonetheless testify to his deep insight into the psychology of gay men in 1920s Europe and the cultural and political atmosphere of the time. And unlike the famous novella written by Mann, who is also a master of irony, Granand's texts are not tragic. Instead, they offer a refreshingly candid, witty, and largely exuberant look at everyday lives. This can perhaps best be seen in "Nemesis": arguably the most sex-positive of the stories, it is the longest of all and occupies a central place in the collection. Astonishingly, the relationship of the protagonists, Trudy and Erich, is casually described at one point —nearly a century before same-sex marriage was legalized in Germany and the U.S.—as a "marriage" ("Ehe").

But Granand's collection is also a tale of suppression, since its successive banning by two separate German courts in 1920 and 1921, when the new government's end of censorship started to be reversed during the Weimar Republic, effectively kept it from public view, apart from occasional, later reprints in gay magazines as described in Manfred Herzer's essay, for over seventy years. One wonders how the availability of these stories—and others like them we may not even know about—might have changed the way gay characters have been depicted in modern literature. Some of the characters, such as Freddy, in "Nocturne," who appears to make his living selling his body, may seem stereotypical now, but while we've become accustomed to seeing female prostitutes depicted in literature and the arts, representations of rent boys, whether stereotyped or sympathetic, are few and far between. Freddy may seem familiar from our early twenty-first century vantage point, where we may encounter similar characters in literature, film, and other media, but there was almost no such image in circulation in Granand's time. The fact that today we have a deeper sense of the interior life of poor and disenfranchised characters lets us appreciate both Granand's prescience and his artistic courage. Likewise, in "Nemesis," we witness detailed and elaborate descriptions of the club scene in 1920s Berlin, replete with the arcane rules for how to enter a space, how to approach others, how to pay for drinks, how to dress, and how to behave appropriately—or not! In this way, Granand reveals an insider perspective, unlike the outsider view of Weimar-era Berlin nightlife found in

Christopher Isherwood's book *Goodbye to Berlin* (set several years after Granand's book and published in 1939) or any of its adaptations, such as John von Druten's *I Am a Camera* (1951), which later became Harold Prince's musical *Cabaret* (1966). But the nuanced, humorous, insider account of the clubs of Weimar Berlin, which catered to a wide range of men from military and working-class backgrounds to the moneyed elite, such as Granand's, has been less available to audiences. Or consider as well in "Nemesis" the scene near the beginning where the protagonists meet in a cruising area in Berlin's Tiergarten park and engage in what the narrator ironically calls the "solemn ceremony" of the cigarette ritual, in which one man stops another to ask for a light, allowing him to gaze into the eyes of the person lighting the match, which is how two gay men in such an area were often able to identify each other as available and establish a safe place.

Rather than viewing Granand's figures, then, as blueprints for future depictions of gay life, they may best be understood as archetypes that reveal an essential truth about human behavior. The burglar seduced by his victim, the musician thought to be betrayed by his lover, the cadet torn between the affection of two superiors, the traveling student emboldened to kiss a naïve American, and the lost son of the bourgeoisie are archetypes of human longing bristling at fate. Since the 1920s, all these characters have been revived and refined in an evolving tradition. A work such as Granand's gives us a road map that indicated some possibilities of what was to come, but in Germany that map was destroyed.

Censorship, of course, was not strictly an issue limited to Germany; nor was gay-themed literature the only target of suppression. It's worth recalling that, despite the quite different political and cultural contexts, in 1921, the year Granand's collection fell victim to the censors in two German courts, the New York Court of Special Session ruled sections of James Joyce's novel *Ulysses* (published in France in 1922) to be obscene, and prohibited its publication in the U.S.

The urge to censor, moreover, frequently leads as well to the curtailment of other freedoms. Perhaps one of the lessons to ponder from the virtual disappearance of Granand's collection is that our various freedoms of expression—of speaking, writing, loving, of openly being ourselves in the evolving norms of our time—are fragile and not to be taken for granted. The banning of books is an ever-present pastime designed by the disingenuous to appeal to the disaffected, which Yeats hauntingly calls, in his poem "The Second Coming," first published in 1920, those "full of passionate intensity." This is especially the case in work depicting or describing the range of human erotic desire. The loss of freedoms may often start with the banning of books but rarely ends with it.

My initial efforts in finding a publisher for an English translation in the mid-90s proved fruitless. Editors thought stories of same-sex love by an obscure German author available only as a reprint after they had been censored and suppressed for over seventy years would not be commercially viable. But I was recently led to return to this project with renewed determination, to turn a tale of suppression into one of survival. For me personally, this narrative arc is appealing as I confront the effects of a stroke suffered by my husband, Marvin, who has championed these stories from the very beginning. The survival of the text is also due to the commitment and persistence of legions of people, many of them outside mainstream culture, academia, and publishing: activists, archivists, and independent scholars who labor at small presses and niche magazines to recover and keep alive what otherwise could be easily and oftentimes deliberately forgotten, suppressed, or lost.

In an essay published in 1923, as a foreword to his German translation of poems by the French symbolist poet Charles Baudelaire (*Tableaux Parisiens*), the German-Jewish philosopher and literary critic Walter Benjamin proposes that a translation offers a "continued life" *(fortleben)*—somewhat different than a mode of "survival" *(überleben)*—to a literary work. In the case of Granand, however, that continued life never properly began since his stories had been twice denied, first by Weimar censors during a period that supposedly provided new freedoms and encouraged experimentation, and later, brutally, by the Nazis, who also forced the author into exile in Brazil. But this suppression means that Granand's work now deserves its chance, with today's readers, at proving its own worth.

As I read the work today—nearly thirty years after having discovered it—I remain impressed by its power to imagine and celebrate a range of possibilities in its depiction of LGBTQ+ life beyond the tragic mode. The world is different today, and yet these stories might inspire and fuel a young reader's search for themselves in ways the censors blocked in 1920 and 1921. The task of cultural preservation and of discovering previously silenced voices is as necessary today as in the 1920s, as our country yet again debates which works of literature to permit and which to suppress. This first English-language edition of Granand's delightful collection enables me, at long last, to share my experience and excitement with new readers, allowing them, in turn, the opportunity to continue the life of Granand's remarkable work.

PROLOGUE

The Little Garden

This little garden is no artfully constructed, well-maintained, stylized park. It has crooked, convoluted, and uncontrolled paths, flowers in the dazzling colors of a farmer's garden, or with riotously fragrant aromas, it has thorns and plenty of weeds. But over it all the great, hot sun shines, the melancholy moon passes by, and the innocent stars twinkle. This garden is a slice of life...

BERLIN GARDEN OF EROTIC DELIGHTS

THE NEMESIS

Tiergarten, the central park in Berlin, near the Brandenburg Gate.

It's July, and there's a full moon, with the air so warm and clammy you could almost grab hold of it, or splash into it, as if it were warm water. It smells of asphalt, gasoline, and horses. On the pathways, shadowy figures (mostly male) scurry along from time to time. Trudy has reached the semicircle by the Brandenburg Gate and heads down a byway. Slender and of medium height with light-blond hair and blue eyes, he's dressed in a sailor's uniform in which his shoulders and hips sway effortlessly, adopting a leisurely way of walking that at any moment could lead him to stand still without drawing any attention. It is the flaneur's well-practiced stride that shows (just as a merchant displays his wares in an easily surveyable and seductive manner) he's available, promises discretion, and guarantees satisfaction. For Trudy knows what he's doing: he keeps his head in the direction he's walking; only his eyes glance discreetly back to the right. For there, maintaining a fairly exact distance, is Erich Gruner, violinist with the Philharmonic Orchestra.

Erich Gruner is already in his late twenties but looks much younger, which in these circles should come as no surprise. He catches up to Trudy on the byway, walking almost next to him for a bit, then says, decisively, "Good evening!"

Trudy, softly and very shyly, replies, "Good evening."

A pause.

Smiling, they silently look each other over; the continuation of the entire adventure hinges on this inspection. There's still time for an honorable retreat, with some such words as "Oh, sorry, I thought you were someone else..."

But Erich Gruner finally says, "What a fabulously beautiful evening."

Trudy has trouble finding the proper response. He asks, "Do you perhaps have a match?" That isn't supposed to mean that he wants something to smoke, since he is already taking a cigarette out of the knot of his sailor's collar. It's just that it would be unthinkable for Trudy to begin an acquaintance in any other way than by the request for a light. It's part and parcel of his style, and any departure from this formula could cause confusion or at least uncertainty.

Erich Gruner lights a match and takes out a cigarette from his case, thus beginning the solemn ceremony of the lighting of the cigarette, including the obligatory gazing into the eyes. They walk along side by side.

By now, Trudy feels free to ask, "Why didn't you say something to me earlier?"

Erich says, laughing, "Well, I had to get a better look at you first!" And with a furtive glance he checks out Trudy one more time and says, "Who knows what might be running around out here."

Trudy, ignoring this last remark, says, "Where should we go?" "I don't know," says Erich, still a bit unsure. "Do you want to go farther into the park?" Trudy asks.

At that moment, they stop in a secluded spot, both hesitating. They try getting to know each other in the darkness. They touch each other. Find each other's hands (very discreetly!). Squeeze them. Lean up against each other. Breathe deeply. Touch each other's foreheads. Feel each other's breath. Kiss. Then they hold each other tight as if they would never let go.

After this wordless scene, Erich Gruner says as if in response to it, "We can take the streetcar to my place, where it's comfortable." "You live on the West Side?" replies Trudy. "Yes, let's go," says Erich. And with that they head out.

Eight days later; it's morning and the weather has become uncomfortably wet as Erich gets ready to leave for rehearsal. He's got everything except his overcoat , which has disappeared. It can't be found anywhere: It's not hanging on its hook in the corridor, nor is it in the bedroom, nor living room nor kitchen. And this covers Erich Gruner's entire realm! The coat must be somewhere in the apartment, yet he can't find it. It's a beautiful blue, stylish summer coat. Just as an aside, Erich Gruner lives on a strict budget!

Now Erich begins talking to himself (like all people who are alone a lot): "It's not possible! It can't be! How could I be so easily taken in?" he says, as he searches further. Eventually, he leaves without his coat, arriving late to rehearsal.

That evening, Erich is expecting Trudy to arrive by 10 p.m. From his experience with him over the past few days, Erich knows Trudy to be timely and reliable, as someone who still has manners, and generally modest and a dear mate. But it gets to be 10:15, Then 10:30, then 11 o'clock, and still he hasn't shown up.

At 11:30, Erich goes to bed, depressed, not because of his coat, whose whereabouts he now knows, but because of his loss of faith in people.

The next day, he writes to Trudy, but the letter is returned as undeliverable. Erich's good friends who hear about the story laugh him off as a hopeless idealist, bent on improving humanity, and a cloud-dwelling dreamer.

Three days later, his friend Georg Braun comes over and orders Erich to go out with him to the Paradise Ballroom. Erich had never been there, out of shyness, but this time he has a premonition and decides to go.

After buying their tickets, each priced at one mark and fifty cents, they enter the packed hall. At the moment, everyone's dancing a slow, intimate waltz, with passionate feeling and piano accompaniment. There are also a few ladies present, dancing among themselves.

All at once, Erich spots Trudy, who in turn notices him. First Trudy laughs, and then quickly turns beet red, but then acts as if he hadn't seen him, seeming entirely absorbed in dancing with a soldier in a field-gray uniform.

Everyone turns slowly and steadily, as if wound up like toys. Trudy seems completely under the sway of the dance, and his gaze seems to be turned entirely inward. But no matter which direction the waltz turns him, his face remains consistently turned away from the spot where Erich stands.

The waltz lasts a long time, and the crowd sings along in unison to several especially popular passages, although they often get the words wrong. Trudy continues dancing with a death-defying attitude. Erich remains quietly in his spot in the background.

Then suddenly the piano stops and the dance breaks off. The couples, content and courteous, head back to their beer tables. Many of the gentlemen wave small fans, less because of the heat than for flirting. There are few starched collars; most wear shirts that leave their chests exposed and have taken off their coats.

Others sport striped, tight-fitting sweaters with scarves around their bare necks. There are many soldiers, from officers on down the ranks. And (of course!) sailors, both real and pretend ones. Some of the gentlemen appear in women's clothing, wearing heavy make-up and displaying touchingly large hands and feet.

The entire scene proceeds very respectably, punctuated only occasionally by a high-pitched scream, or squeal.

The dance floor is now deserted. At the beer tables, everyone's wiping the perspiration from their brows, necks, and arms with large colored handkerchiefs. A woman selling flowers finds many customers for her pink carnations. Ah! There is still gallantry in the world!

But Trudy has disappeared.

Erich sits down at a table with Georg, not saying anything and looking around the hall anxiously. Georg nudges him: "Say something. Don't you like it here?" Erich, somewhat awkwardly, says, "Yeah, sure." Georg, in high spirits and completely into the scene, replies, "Come on, man! Later we'll dance together. Cheers!"

Now comes the foxtrot.

The first note from the piano electrifies the men. Almost everyone's on their feet. They pair off and run around like crazy, lifting up their knees as high as they'll go. They next form a circle, break back down into pairs, and then reform the circle. The result is a convulsive, trancelike writhing, causing the whole room to shake and pulsate in two-four time. It makes you think of India and fakirs, and at any moment someone might drop down dead. Even the few real women dutifully take up the dance.

Suddenly, Trudy, with his soldier, is back among the dancers. He moves about wildly full of holy zeal, swinging his arms and legs like mad: foxtrot! His expression conveys one thing only: foxtrot!

Erich stands in a corner; in this pulsating whirl of humanity, his eyes steadily follow Trudy's sailor's cap as it bounces up and down on his head. Then the piano player stops, and the bewitched crowd, freed from its frenzied state, takes back its places at the tables.

Erich sees Trudy's sailor's cap flutter through the exit. In a flash, he's right behind him, and before they get very far, he grabs hold of Trudy, who's panting from having danced so ecstatically and determined to go outside even though it's raining, which could cause the maritime bronze that he'd applied to his face to run and ruin his beautifully crimped hair and generally put an end to all beauty everywhere. Trudy is intent on not realizing who's grabbed him, but Erich holds him firmly.

Seeing no way out of it, Trudy says, with poorly feigned surprise, "Oh, you're here?"

Erich, with genuine concern, replies, "Don't go out into the cold rain after you've danced yourself into a sweat. Be reasonable!" But Trudy continues struggling to break free, saying, "Oh please...I gotta cool down."

They go together out into the rain when Erich realizes he won't be able to hold onto Trudy much longer. What he'd like to say now is "Where's my coat?" But at the last moment he thinks that maybe, or perhaps he only hopes, that it's not true, that the coat is hanging somewhere at home. And, anyway, he wants to spare him the humiliation of such an inquisition, for by coming into direct contact with him he falls under Trudy's spell. So he just asks, "Why didn't you come over the other evening?"

Trudy, embarrassed, looks around nervously: "Oh, I wasn't able to make it." But Erich doesn't let the subject drop: "And yesterday and the day before that you couldn't come either...Listen, I have something to talk to you about. When can you come over?" Trudy breathes a sigh of relief: "I'll come over tomorrow night…definitely! Trust me, I'll be there by 10." Trudy then frees himself and starts to go. Erich holds out his hand: "Good-bye." Trudy, hesitating, takes hold of Erich's hand, saying, "Good-bye," and disappears into the rain.

In the ballroom, the dancing goes on, when the announcer shouts: "Take up your places for the Tirolean." Couple after couple take their places behind one another until the line reaches around the room. Then the pianist lets loose, in mazurka time. Erich leans up against the wall, not paying much attention, but then gradually perks up at what he sees. The dance unfolds before him like a spectacle as a common rhythm animates all the couples. They take a few steps forward on the mazurka beat, clinging to each other. Next, one of them raises his right hand, holding onto the partner's, when the "girl" twirls herself around once under the man's right hand, thus completing the movement. All of this is performed with as much grace and refinement as possible, for this is a genuine, formal salon dance. And yet the most beautiful part occurs before the movement is repeated, when the "girl," having twirled herself around, swings herself forward to the male partner of the couple just ahead. The dance lasts just as long as it takes the girls to make their round once and then end up back with their original partners.

It's not this delicate choreography, though, that so interests Erich, but rather the field-gray soldier who Trudy had been dancing with and who now, after Trudy's flight, is dancing with others. The soldier soon becomes aware that Erich keeps looking over his way and therefore dances with particular elegance and precision. And every time his partner twirls around on his right hand, he glances at Erich, as if to say, "See how beautifully I can do that!" For Erich is, after all, a highly desirable catch, a person one would gladly flirt with. (Especially because this crowd makes his clothing seem doubly elegant, but also because he himself does indeed look more than passable.)

Gradually, the soldier's glance turns into a smile, to which Erich, whether out of courtesy or calculation, smiles back; at the conclusion of the Tirolean, and in true chivalric fashion, the soldier requests the next dance of Erich, who responds by asking if he would like a glass of beer. When they sit down at their table, Erich tells him that he doesn't dance, so the soldier quickly engages him in conversation: "Do you go to the balls often?" "No, this is my first time," says Erich. "I guess you haven't been in Berlin very long then?" says the soldier. "On the contrary, four years," replies Erich. The soldier shakes his head; he can't believe it: "I've never seen you around at all before. But tonight's not that interesting. The day after tomorrow, you need to go to the Diana Ballroom; there, you'll really see something. Not the tacky get-ups you find here, but real ball outfits, including lace trimmings. You can't even tell they're drag queens. And people running around coatless, well, you won't find that at Diana, either."

In the meantime, the Rhinelander has begun. The soldier's stream of words has dried up, and his eyes wander to the couples dancing. But because he knows what's proper, he stays next to his gentleman friend, fending off invitations to dance with tactful references to Erich. Erich catches on to the etiquette: "Please, go ahead! I don't want to keep you from having fun just because I don't dance." The soldier and his dance partner thank Erich with a bow, and every time they pass by Erich, the soldier nods to him. Which means: "Even though I'm now dancing with someone else, I belong to you."

When the dance is over, both the soldier and his dancer thank Erich, just as courtesy and good manners demand. And it is nice when courtesy and good manners ennoble even common interactions!

Now everyone starts dancing the Hiawatha, a bold, heroic, spirited number. A chorus often breaks in, especially at the passage:

> "Lights off! Knives out!
> Hit 'em till sparks fly about..."

or the tender lines:

> "And it's all because of you!
> And it's all because of you!"

Meanwhile, the atmosphere in the hall has intensified. Poetry also lives in beer—it doesn't always have to be wine! A few glasses are enough to lend a certain aura to life. With a bit of alcohol in your veins, you see the everyday through multicolored glass. In short, a Dionysian delight and heedlessness rules: People kiss in the corners and sit on one another's laps. Some, forgetful of the world, their lives, and everything else that exists, sit close together, silently holding hands, gazing into their partners' eyes. They get up, like sleepwalkers, only when a new song begins, and then they dance some more, retaining their intimate embrace.

Here, there are no lies! Here is simple humanity, all poor sinners if you like, doing what they cannot help and being who they are.

Erich looks over at a couple lingering somewhere deep in Elysium, and he suddenly experiences vivid pangs thinking about Trudy. Then, diplomatically, he quizzes the soldier: "By the way, where's the sailor you were dancing with?" "He left," the soldier replies. Erich has to make a new start: "I think I know him. Is his name Rudi?" "Yeah, yeah," says the soldier, "his name's Rudi…or Trudy!" Erich says, "But I've totally forgotten his last name," and he makes as though he's trying to come up with it. But the soldier just says (not sounding quite convincing), "I don't know his last name either. We all call him Trudy."

This conversation hits a dead end, but Erich doesn't give up easily. They have another beer, and then he waltzes with the soldier, who cuddles up to him as they dance, becoming steadily more intimate.

Erich picks up where he left off, with a laugh and shaking his head (and as an aside, of course): "Why did Trudy just suddenly leave so early?" Which is supposed to mean: "It's so nice here and I can't understand why anyone would leave so early."

The soldier bends over close to him, wrinkles his brow, and says very softly: "Yeah, he said to me earlier that we should go to the Brandenburg Gate. I said to him, 'What, not out in the rain!' And he said, 'Yeah, I took something from someone who just got here, so I don't want to stick around.' I said to him, 'Oh, stay here, we're having a good time; he's not going after you here…' and the next thing I know, he's gone."

Erich doesn't know how to respond. After a while, he says, "Oh well," and then, after another pause, "That's how it goes!" But now he can think that there's no longer any doubt that Trudy had stolen the coat. Trudy, who he had as much as lived with for a whole week!

Just then someone shouts to the soldier, "Paulie, come on, let's do the slide." As the soldier dances, Erich sits alone at the table. By this time almost all the lovebirds have left, but the ones who have hung on keep dancing like crazy.

When the slide is over, the electric lights turn off, and a murky morning light streams in through the windows, making all the faces, which had only recently appeared so fresh and youthful, look wilted and tired.

The piano player gets up and leaves while the bartender claps his hands and shouts: "Gentlemen, it's closing time!" To prevent one of the guests from starting yet another dance, he locks the piano cover while his crew clears the tables and puts up the chairs.

Finally the guests themselves are driven from the hall like a flock of sheep.

Outside, gray misery blankets the street. It's damp, windy, and grimy. The streetcar isn't running yet, and there are no longer any cabs to be found at this godforsaken hour. To get to the West Side takes an hour and a half by foot. The soldier and Erich walk a little way together arm in arm; the soldier cuddles up to him, just like during the waltz, while Erich sings in march tempo: "And it's all because of you! And it's all because of you!" The soldier rocks gently to the rhythm. "In eight days there's going to be another dance at the Paradise Ballroom," says the soldier. "You're gonna go to that one too?" Erich shrugs his shoulders, "I don't know yet." The soldier presses up even closer against Erich: "Ah, come on!" In saying this, he takes hold of Erich's hand, squeezes it, sighs heavily and says, having bent his head over closer to Erich and looking him in the eyes: "bubbe!"

Which means, translated into the language of great novels, about as much as "I love you!"

Erich doesn't quite know what to do. Truth be told, the soldier's solicitations have in fact aroused his vanity. Which is what happens when the first blush of youth is behind you! But then he's also overcome with compassion, for he knows very well that the soldier's efforts will be in vain. In the end, however, he genuinely starts to like the soldier. This simple person who is opening himself up without any inhibitions has something in his very being that is immensely honest, transparent, and matter-of-fact. Something that convinces and captivates you. And Erich, who is a rather complicated person, has a great longing for simplicity.

But just as the laws of love and lust do not correspond to the knowledge of the good, just as love is often a perfectly malicious, wicked, foolish bird, so sympathy and admiration cannot now light a fire in Erich, and his love, just as it had before, makes him long for the cursed sailor who robbed him. So he replies to the soldier's offer as innocuously as possible: "Hey, I'm not a boy anymore." But the soldier does not want to hear that. Instead, he says: "My boy, come with me." "But we're both really too tired, you know," says Erich. "Now, bubbe, I'll get you home," says the soldier. "You don't have to worry about it. And if you don't want to get together tonight, I won't come up, and we'll meet up another time." As he says all this, he's frantically squeezing Erich's hand and now starts groping him.

Suddenly someone behind them shouts from about a block away: "Hey, Paulie! Where are you going?" Annoyed, the soldier replies, "Shut your trap, horseface! Mind your own business!" And he turns back to Erich, saying softly, "Isn't that right, bubbe?"

But Erich decides to get to the point, if also as gently as possible: "You see, don't take this the wrong way…but I have a boyfriend…" The soldier stops short, and in a big-hearted, cheerful tone, says, "Go on, bubbe."

"Well, that sailor we'd been speaking about is actually my boyfriend," says Erich, "and, well, perhaps he's told you that he's stolen something from someone…" Erich pauses, and so the soldier says, encouragingly, "Yeah, he told me that." "You see," says Erich, "I'm the one he stole from…my coat. And even after we'd already become very close friends."

The soldier, taken aback, says, "He stole something from you?"

The soldier would consider the crime itself to be a trivial matter, not anything even to think about when it doesn't happen to you, and also because it's not such a big deal to pinch something sometimes. Good lord, it's really nothing! Happens all the time! But the crime grows in importance, even becoming an unpardonable offense, now that it touches on the soldier's personal circle of friends. He can't help but blurt out, "That lowlife scumbag!" And then, like a knight ready to defend his lord, "Don't worry, bubbe, I'll take care of this. He'll get what's coming to him."

Erich has conflicting feelings. He's almost sorry for betraying Trudy, yet hopes that the soldier's intervention might give rise to some good. And so for now, the conversation between Erich and the soldier loses interest...

And it can be taken as self-evident that the next evening, despite having promised to come over, Trudy fails to appear at Erich's place.

On Saturday evening, Erich shows up around 11 p.m. at the Diana Ballroom. The Diana is completely different from the Paradise Ballroom. First of all, it boasts a beautiful room with high ceilings and ornate architecture in the Empire style. A hall whose formal nobility puts anything on the West Side of Berlin to shame. Here, you could imagine your great-grandmothers taking their first, virginal dance steps at the choral society balls. Then a real string orchestra plays on a brightly colored stage that has been built into the hall with a studied nonchalance. And finally, the guests are decidedly upscale (it cost five marks to get in!). Soldiers and working class guys are distinctly in the minority, while choice attire, pleated trousers, and cologne prevail. The better area of the city, including the Tauentzien Boulevard, is well-represented, as well as that world that thrives on gossip.

Just as Erich enters the hall, a call goes out for the Tirolean dance, and from the sea of humanity that is present the first couples rush to line up behind one another. As fate would have it, the "girl" of number three is none other than Trudy. Trudy in his blue sailor's uniform, radiating, carefree, and on the hand of someone wearing a high stiff-collar cutaway, an elegant pince-nez, and rings on his fingers—in short, on the hand of a gentleman. But this time, Trudy, who's making polite conversation, has not noticed Erich's arrival.

And while the couples continue lining up, Erich conceives of a bold battle plan. He approaches a young man, who, beautifully painted and more than elegantly dressed, and possessing the modesty expected of a young girl, is waiting for a dance partner. Erich leads him by the hand as they join the other couples while the music soon fills the room. He knows the Tirolean from his evening at the Paradise Ballroom. He knows its strict, invariable law, that the "girl," after every completed dance figure, is given over to the male dancer of the next couple until ultimately she ends up with her original partner. And Erich knows that the revenge which has eluded him will deliver Trudy—the nemesis he trusted!—into his arms.

The dance moves along. Erich's already had eight different girls in his arms, and there are many more to come before he gets to Trudy because there are so many couples. Trudy is still far away.

Every new girl contributes, so to speak, a new nuance to the dance, and Erich finds himself as if surrounded by drowning people as he gets rocked about in the tumult. At one moment he has to carry a heavy burden, at the next he himself is lifted up. Some girls are completely uninterested in him and look back longingly toward their original partner while others happily embrace each new find. The old and the young, the revolting and the rosy-cheeked, the beautifully perfumed and those doused in the smells of Berlin. Sometimes a real woman appears as well, but only very seldom!

In the meantime, Trudy, getting ever closer to Erich, suddenly catches sight of him. Trudy had been fully absorbed in the Tirolean, but now he turns first bright red, then completely white again, while his legs keep moving to the beat of the mazurka and his arms glide, trancelike, into those of his new partner's; his spirit, though, is no longer into the dance. Just a moment ago each fiber of his heart had surrendered to the formal steps of the Tirolean, but now he carries them out like a well-trained circus animal.

His expression gradually grows dark while he racks his brains trying to figure out how to escape, but he's lost precious time as only a few couples remain left between him and Erich.

The dance unwinds like a fateful thread, and as in an ancient tragedy, the frightful nemesis hustles up ever closer to Trudy until, when there is only one couple left between the two of them, Trudy cracks a smile. A lifeless, helpless smile that says, "whatever happens, happens!" And with this smile Trudy ends up in Erich's arms and as they dance, Erich nods slightly and says, "Hello, Trudy."

Trudy clears his throat and then says, with a parched voice, "Oh! You're here again!"

But as he holds Trudy tightly in his arms, Erich observes how Trudy's chest, lying open under his sailor's collar, beats violently. This tan, sturdy chest that bears a tattoo of a rising sun whose rays shine far up into his neck and whose full, round disk lies in a sparkling little spot of sea, reminding him of how this sun had transformed seven long nights into absolutely luminous days.

And so, suddenly Erich—although he certainly hadn't intended it in the accusation he'd planned in his head so carefully—turns soft and says to Trudy, "Rudi, my darling. Why can't you believe in me?" With a slight, barely perceptible nod of the head, Trudy seems to be preparing an answer, but at this moment the music dictates that the couples break up. Then comes the circle, around which Trudy has to dance by himself, precluding any further discussion; after that, he has to move on to the next dancer.

For a moment, Erich's cause seems lost. But soon the most astonishing thing happens.

The Tirolean is over, clearing the dance hall, and everyone gathers round the tables in the adjoining rooms. Erich, feeling a bit lost among the throngs, heads over there too, when suddenly Trudy, tugging at Erich's arm, whispers in a hoarse voice, "Can I speak to you for a minute?" They then go out to the entrance hall, a place where one usually is careful not to engage in intimate conversation. Taking a deep breath, Trudy quickly says, "I took your coat. But it's still at home. I haven't done anything to it. I just didn't dare come to see you again." And he looks at Erich with a sad expression.

And now that Erich seems to have the better of him, he becomes stern, to teach him a lesson. Moreover, he still doesn't quite trust Trudy and thus replies carefully: "Yeah, so?" Which prompts Trudy to try to excuse himself: "It happened so fast. The coat was hanging there as I was leaving, and in that moment...I just took it!"

Trudy waits to see how Erich would react to his words, but he remains unmoved and does not reply. Trudy continues even more intensely: "As soon as I got outside, it struck me what I'd done. But the front door had already closed shut. And the concierge was standing on the staircase. I didn't know what else I could do and just took off. I'll give your coat back tomorrow, or, or," and his face lights up, "should we go to my place now and pick it up?"

Somewhat mischievously, Erich asks: "Where do you live, anyway, Trudy?"

Trudy, now again feeling intimidated, says: "Yeah, I lied to you about that, too. I've not understood how you could be so good to me. I never thought we'd get together more than once; that's just not how it goes with pickups in the park. Most don't want to know anything at all about you. You're just good enough for someone to take you home, once. So when you asked for my address, right on the first day, I gave you a false one. Then as I got to know you better, I was too embarrassed to tell you that I'd lied."

Erich is serious now: "But as you ran off with the coat, it didn't occur to you that we could meet each other again?" Trudy shrugs his shoulders: "I wasn't thinking of anything at all. I simply didn't want to think about it anymore."

"I could have reported you to the police; they would have found you."

Trudy stares at the floor: "Yes, that's true…it just goes on." Which is his way of saying, "I guess it's just my lot to be who I am and to do what I do."

Erich suddenly glimpses into an abyss.

Something then hits Erich: "You dance without any care in the world, seem to go to all the balls, take walks in the Tiergarten park. Don't you work at all?"

Trudy laughs bitterly: "Oh, I never got very far in school. I did have an apprenticeship, but then the war came, everyone was excited, including me. I enlisted in the navy because that's what my three brothers did. They're all dead: Two were killed in action, one died at sea. And me, I'm sitting here now."

Laying his hand on Trudy's shoulder, Erich says, "Don't you know anyone who can help you out?" Trudy shakes his head no.

"Rudi, you were just saying something about people you

know whom you've met in the Tiergarten, that they never want anything more than to amuse themselves with you and then don't care about you after that. Why do you go there at all, then?"

Trudy bursts out bitterly: "I can't even go there anymore. Paul, the soldier who was with you the other night at the Paradise, he's already told everyone the story about the coat. This afternoon, when I got to the gate, right away two of them screamed, 'Hey, Trudy, where's your new coat?' Then they say the next time I should bring them one, too. They only do that of course because they want to snatch away all the gentlemen for themselves."

"Why do you go to that cruising spot at all then," Erich asks.

Trudy pauses, feeling very embarrassed, but then looks at Erich straight in the eye: "It's not to make money! I still get my unemployment checks and keep on trying to find a job. It's just that I can't stand being always alone. And I can't start nothing with women... I keep swearing I'll never go cruising again, but then..."

Breaking off suddenly, Trudy goes from a defensive to a combative posture. "Hey, you go cruising there, too!"

Erich has to laugh and shakes his head: "Actually, I don't. That we met there at all was more a matter of chance. The weather was so gorgeous that I walked from the Philharmonic to the streetcar. But"—and here his voice trembles—"when I saw you, Rudi, I followed you."

Then Trudy says softly: "I'm always thinking that when I go to the park or to the balls, I tell myself, maybe this time you'll find a real boyfriend." For quite some time, they gaze into each other's eyes. Then, Trudy looks down again and says, "And that was so idiotic of me to take your coat after you'd been so good to me." "Yes, it was very stupid," says Erich.

Trudy, gradually speaking more freely, "But I wouldn't have dared ever to talk to you again until today I realized that we'd probably keep running into each other and that I'd never have any peace, and then, as we were dancing together, suddenly I realized that I needed to talk to you. I decided I'd give the coat back to you, and if you didn't want nothing more to do with me, well, then I wouldn't bother you no more."

He looks at Erich with his large sailor's eyes, and the rays of the rising sun tattooed on his chest shine invitingly and seductively while from the dance hall can be heard the muted sounds of a devilishly sensuous waltz. At that moment, it's as if the entrance hall and all the people standing around disappear, and as if everything earthly dissolves into a gray mist and these two beloved children, defying all the principles of a proper upbringing, enclose in a deep embrace and a long, passionate kiss, sending them heavenward. Finally, as if in a dream, they stagger into the hall and join in the waltz.

They waltz, however, as if the dance were not taking place on a Berlin parquet floor, but as if they experienced all the wonder of their immense, fervid, dazzling love under the glare of the rising sun on Trudy's sailor's breast.

They would have certainly remained reeling in this state of intoxication if it were not for the appearance of two people who brought them back to reality: Paul, the soldier, and Georg Braun, Erich's skeptical friend, both of whom in the meantime had come to the Diana Ballroom and who now, each deeply astonished in his own way, observe this unheard of caprice of fate.

Georg Braun takes Erich aside and offers some well-meaning advice: "Are you never going to wise up? Someday you'll be cleaned out of everything you have!"

"Oh, I've long since had my coat back, it was all just a mistake."

The soldier, meanwhile, asks his question soundlessly, with his mouth wide open and his eyes frozen open in astonishment.

Erich lays his hand tenderly on his arm, and says, "Rudi has come to his senses; everything's okay now. Please tell that to the others, too, the ones you'd already told about the coat. You see, Trudy and I, we're boyfriends after all. But I'm happy to have met you and hope we see each other again often!"

But the soldier, being a gentleman, would never intrude into someone else's marriage, and says, as befits a civilized person, "I'm also real happy to have made your honorable acquaintance."

Whereupon Erich invites the soldier and Georg Braun to tea on Sunday afternoon and, as a sign of the happy ending of this story, dances a proud, heroic Hiawatha with the soldier.

But after that, Trudy and Erich leave the ballroom and speed away in a roaring automobile as if on clouds to the West Side and Erich Gruner's little kingdom, whose nocturnal darkness will soon be brightened by the rising sun.

The next day, Trudy returns the coat. He never goes back to the Brandenburg Gate, and he and Erich have become lovers.

NOCTURNE

FREDDY'S BEDROOM. WALLS AND FURNITURE ARE WHITE; THE wide brass bed is covered with a violet silk spread turned back halfway. Delicate violet silk curtains are pulled closed over the window. A brownish-gray carpet. In front of the bed a small, very bright prayer rug. On the walls, Japanese woodcuts in slender silver frames. A small, dark Louis XVI dressing table with inlays stands on a white fur in front of the window; on it, between two silver lamps, a silver mantel clock and miscellaneous jewelry. In a small crystal tray is an attractive jumble of gold cufflinks studded with small diamonds, tie tacks, rings with beautifully sparkling stones, bracelets made of platinum and gold—everything a bit flashy and, for a young man, which Freddy after all is, also a tad over the top. But for Freddy, these things are absolutely no luxuries but more like necessities of life, or, to put it another way, the trappings of his profession.

A small antique Venetian chandelier is illuminated overhead.

Freddy stands barefoot in light silk pajamas in front of the dressing table, manicuring his fingernails. He's very slim and of average height. His hair, blond and full, is brushed back. His eyebrows are thin, arched high, and colored fairly dark.

The clock strikes three.—He casts a casual glance at the clock and sprays himself with cologne. Then he walks slowly over to the nightstand, turns on a small, violet-shaded lamp, takes a cigarette out of a silver case, lights it with a lighter, turns off the chandelier, and climbs into bed.

Now for a few moments it is completely still. The room is only dimly illuminated in violet. Freddy, lying on his back, his eyes half shut, smokes his cigarette.

Then the door opens slowly and soundlessly. A bullseye lantern becomes visible. A burglar slips in silently. He's rather tall and broad-shouldered, wearing a tight-fitting, blue-white, horizontally striped cotton shirt that reveals a well-defined chest and leaves his neck and arms free. Dark trousers, loose around the hips, taper down to the ankles and are held up from above by a leather belt. He wears felt shoes. On his head is a round black balloon cap, pulled far down over his face, which is beardless and tanned. His movements are slow and halting; with each step he rocks his entire body.

He slowly scans the room with his lantern. Freddy, still enveloped in some kind of violet dreams, suddenly starts up, "Ah..."

The burglar shines his lantern on him, and with one glance at the look on Freddy's face, feels himself master of the situation. Softly but firmly he says, "Scuse me fur trublin' ya."

Then neither of them moves for a few moments as they size each other up.

Freddy, whose mouth has by now become quite dry, and after trying a few times to swallow, implores the bullseye lantern (for that's all he can see), "What do you want?"

The burglar, preternaturally calm and with the grand gesture of a gentleman from one of the oldest parts of Munich, says, "I'm sleepwalkin', ya know!"

Freddy, still blinded by the lantern, says, "You won't find anything here."

The burglar, condescending but good-natured, replies, "Dat so?...Lemme see for myself."

He puts the lantern down on a small table where the light

shines directly onto Freddy. Then he goes to the middle of the room, stands with his back against the bed, stretches his chest until his shoulders rise up to his ears, swings his legs back and forth to loosen his knee joints, and hitches up his trousers by the belt.

During all this Freddy tries quietly to get up.

But the burglar has ears trained expressly for his profession. He can also see what goes on behind his back without having to turn around, and therefore says, as if incidentally, "Pleez, don't strain yourself. I can handle it myself."

To which Freddy, feeling dead tired, says, "Yes, but what is it you want, anyway?" And then, looking up at the burglar like a wounded doe, almost pleading: "I told you, you won't find anything…"

The burglar calmly replies, "I know what Im doin'," as he opens the closet and examines the suits, saying, "Nuttin here!"

In the stillness that dominates the room, Freddy can clearly hear the rustling sound as the visitor's coarse hands brush over the silk lining of his suits. At the same time, however, Freddy feels relieved that the burglar's attention has wandered away from him and toward the contents of his closet. The search, which demonstrates not only professional expertise but also conscientiousness, seems to totally absorb the burglar. Which is why suddenly there arises in Freddy a burst of courage that takes even him by surprise. He leaps up and lunges for the door.

The burglar reacts to this by making just a very slight jerky movement toward Freddy, transforming Freddy into a stiff, pale statue even before he has reached the doorknob, but which otherwise doesn't interrupt the burglar's search of the closet. The burglar adds, matter-of-factly, "I awready cut da cord to da fone."

Then he stops what he's doing to say with great satisfaction, "Jeez, a twenty still stickin' in da vest pocket. I'll bet ya forgot 'bout dat." He lays the twenty Mark bill on the small table next to the lantern: "I'll just put it here fur now."

Meanwhile, Freddy, with an air of regal resignation, has moved over to the dressing table. But as he grabs hold of the edge of the table to support himself, heroic thoughts possess him once again. With trembling hands, but with a look of last resolve, he tries turning the key to open the drawer.

But the burglar also foils this effort with a calm, matter-of-fact remark, "Com' on, leave it inside, da gun."—He himself then pulls out a Browning from his pants pocket and cocks it.

This maneuver causes the key, which Freddy, from fright, had pulled out, to slip from his fingers and sink into the thick polar bear fur. With that, Freddy abandons the fight of his life, and along with it also leaving behind the small and big hopes and joys of life, as it were, and, now gliding into the state of resignation before the release of death, drifts back slowly and silently to his bed.

The burglar, Browning in hand, says, "Wot else ya have dats nice?"

Freddy, who is now transfigured and far removed from everything earthly, says, "Take my watch…there…and here, my ring."—He slips off the ring, with its beautiful, large, turquoise stone, and lays it in the burglar's hand, who accepts it in a businesslike manner, as if he had just purchased it. But the nearness of Freddy's tender hand disorients the burglar—if only for a brief moment—from which he quickly recovers. A feeling, shall we say, that does not enter his consciousness any further but nonetheless moves him to utter the words, "Jeez, a tiny hand…like a girl's"—but otherwise does nothing to distract him from his job. For whoever calls himself a genuine burglar can't let himself be led astray by momentary eruptions, whether of sentiments or puzzling feelings, but rather he needs to stay true to his profession and steer a straight course toward the goal of his task. Thus he carefully places the watch and the ring next to the twenty Mark bill on the small table.

Meanwhile the small, silver mantelpiece clock strikes a quarter past the hour, and in doing so betrays its presence.

The burglar glides coolly over to it, "That's wurt sumtin too, eh?...I could take it, too," as he puts it on the small table with the rest. "Ya know, I like order!"

He smiles. His teeth sparkle white. Such quick work is satisfying. In this happy mood he takes inventory of the precious items in the small crystal bowl, rapidly but confidently assessing their value.

Freddy—since life, after all, does not quite as easily surrender to death and transfiguration and makes ever new efforts to assert itself—Freddy, in the face of this deployment of his crown jewels on the table, which resembles the last, sorrowful parade of his faithful guard, and in the face of the burglar's ever-threatening Browning, has been plunged into breathless tension and fear. Looking pale, and with his mouth hanging open, he follows the burglar's every move.

But this gaze affects the burglar somehow. And again, without being aware of it, he is led astray from the straight and narrow path of the performance of carrying out his task, which his profession demands, and a bit diverted speaks, as it were, "off duty." Because even a burglar is a human being, after all! So he says, in a friendly manner: "Why're you lookin' like dat?...I won't do nuttin to ya. Look, we got our laws, and when you don't get in the way of work, yur left in peace."

With that he lays his revolver on the small table, goes over to the dressing table, opens the drawer with a picklock (not deigning to retrieve the key from the fur on the floor), and takes out Freddy's revolver, laying it, too, on the small table. "So....We're even!" He then takes a gentlemanly-like bow with a properly sweeping movement of his right hand that would look good in high society.

This eases up the tension a bit. The tempo of the scene now resembles a cantilena. Freddy, resigning himself again to the situation, takes a book from his nightstand and pretends to be reading.

The burglar, now having been diverted from performing his duty, exhales a certain seductive geniality: "Hey, some cig'rettes!" He takes the cigarette case and, starting to pull one out for himself, suddenly recalls his manners, "Oh...scuse me!" and first offers the cigarettes to Freddy. "You're welcome."

"Thanks," Freddy says drily.

The burglar: "May I...?" He lights a cigarette for himself.

Freddy watches him in astonishment.

Just then he becomes aware that there's something attractive about the dark night visitor, something that fear and dread had previously obscured but which that same fear and dread now seems to heighten, sending a cold shudder through Freddy's body. His eyes remain transfixed on the burglar. Perhaps they are no longer filled with amazement but rather with interest. And on the other side, too, there seems to have been a change toward a pastoral mode.

The burglar, probably trying to gingerly evade a situation he's not able to cope with (for gingerly is one of the most sacred terms of this profession!), looks around gently and says: "Nice place he has here...and looks just like a girl."

Taking advantage of the minor key into which the atmosphere has momentarily modulated, and at the same time suppressing with cool reason (which is for him doubly admirable) the romantic eruptions that have even just now crept up on him, Freddy says, almost calmly, "If you leave now, I won't press charges."

The reference to "pressing charges" rubs the burglar the wrong way. He dismisses it brusquely: "You'd not do nuttin like dat."

Freddy, immediately feeling uncertain again, says, "Why wouldn't I?"

"'Cause you'd not have no peace...Ya know, I know all 'bout ya." Then, speaking in formal German: "We have our detectives, too...Whoever gets on our wrong side will see how it goes then!...Otherwise, we ain't such bad guys at all!"—He then catches sight of Freddy's wallet on the nightstand: "Oh, da wallet, can't furget dat."

Freddy now struggles inwardly with an undeniable and increasingly stubborn sympathy for his visitor along with his aversion to and fear of him. Had there not just been the incident with the wallet, he'd have almost forgotten that he was dealing with a thief. He would have very much liked to have forgotten! But now, being so forcefully reminded of it again, he could only try to finesse the situation, and he passes on to another topic. "By the way, how old are you?"

"Twenne."

The coincidence delights Freddy. "That makes us the same age." He extends the conversation: "But why aren't you in the military?"

The burglar lets out a short laugh. "Yeah, if I'd only gon' in," he says, while flexing his muscles and letting them ripple.

Freddy, feeling increasingly uninhibited, says, "You've such a beautiful body, you could work as a model.—He then goes straight up to him and caresses the muscles on his arm. "You must be incredibly strong." The burglar stretches all his joints and, strutting like a peacock, says: "You'd better believe it!"

"And in great shape," says Freddy.

"Of course I am," the burglar says, and then asks, "Why're ya shakin' like dat? I told ya, I ain't gonna do nuttin to ya."

Cautiously, Freddy says, "I'd like to be just as strong as you....How a person could feel then."

Embarrassed, the burglar laughs, sliding his cap back and forth across his head.

This is the moment when the dramatic crisis occurs. The burglar's abandonment of his path of duty now comes home to haunt him. It's as if the ground on which he's struggling is gradually giving way; or as if he were a fish that now had to swim on land. And to the same degree that he sinks in his role as a highly skilled and vastly experienced burglar, Freddy rises up, ever surer of himself, shifting the conversation and the entire scenario into his very own, innate domain.

But the burglar still isn't aware of the net he's become entangled in, while Freddy is not yet master of the game. Both are like sleepwalkers just following a mysterious something that impels them forward.

Freddy is the first one able to utter a word. "You know, it's too bad that we didn't get to know each other under different circumstances."

"Yeah, wot can ya do 'bout it now?"

"I just really like you," Freddy says.

The burglar, who's not at all suspicious, but rather like a soldier accepting the attentions of his female cook, says, "Really, now!"

Freddy pulls out his arm from one of his pajama sleeves and holds it next to the burglar's, saying, "Look at the difference!"

The burglar says, good-naturedly: "You're nice."—He taps Freddy's arm: "Yes, and such soft skin!...and all silk...Look at my shirt."—He takes Freddy's hand and lays it against his chest.—Then he says, almost astonished, "Hey, yur still shakin'!"

Just then something prevents him from talking or thinking any further. His eyes close automatically. At last, he whispers: "Ya haf nice cologne…"

Breathing a sigh of relief, Freddy says, "I'll get some for you," and starts up toward the dressing table.

But the burglar gathers his wits, and, just as a cat would a mouse, he catches Freddy with both arms and holds him tight, saying, "Yeah, sure, so someone can tell wher' I been t'night."

He has wrapped both hands around Freddy to keep him there.

Then something even stronger than the cologne comes over him. Now he does more than just inhale a devilishly seductive scent; his large, calloused hands, the hands that can break open locks and bash down doors, the hands created for nothing other than breaking and entering, these thoroughly professional hands cradle a small body so soft and lithe and delicate as a—yes, the dutiful burglar who up until now had always put his profession before his personal desires has, despite his twenty years, never had anything so tender in his hands! Why then couldn't a twenty-year-old burglar be virtuous and innocent. The case is rare, but surely it must happen!

Now, holding Freddy in an embrace, the burglar says, "Jesses, he's a small one, and so soft"…

In Freddy, however, powerful images awaken of Carmen, of Circe, of Santuzza.—"You are especially strong."

"D'want me to squeez' a bit?" the burglar suddenly asks.

"Yes," says Freddy.

The burglar hesitates. A tiny part of self-awareness remains in him. But the certain something commands him categorically to squeeze. And while holding him ever more firmly, he still asks,

"D'want me to?"

Freddy, feeling completely aroused, addresses him familiarly, "Yes, just squeeze!"

The burglar now squeezes Freddy firmly up against himself with his arms, asking, "Duz't hurt?"

Freddy, although he can scarcely breathe, says "no!"

The burglar, now squeezing with all his might and without thinking, asks, "Duz't hurt now?"

"No," Freddy moans.

"But it haz ta hurt now," says the burglar, although he means something completely different that he cannot say, letting his words just run their course right at the periphery of what is happening.

And also Freddy means something completely different and yet has to say: "No, no!"

But this "no, no" may have sounded a bit too weak. In any case, a feeling of pity awakens in the burglar, or maybe compassion, certainly some new, previously unknown feeling. And so he asks suddenly, showing great concern, "Ain't ya had enuf yet? Look how hard Im squeezin' ya!"

And as the burglar slowly eases his grip, Freddy lies powerlessly in his arms.

The burglar asks, gently, "Oh…did I squeez' ya too hard?"

Freddy, breathing freely again, smiles for the first time and says, "No…"

The burglar laughs and says, "Dat was nice, huh?"

But Freddy now sees the burglar with new eyes, how he laughs and holds him so happily and how he stands so beautiful and wild and strong before him, that he would really like to tell the burglar just how beautiful and wild and strong he is.—But instead he just remarks, "You have fabulous strength."

And the burglar, who actually has no longer been a burglar for some time now, but rather a poor fool wrenched away from his familiar path and profession, lingers with Freddy. "Yur gettin' yur color back."—Holding him now with only one arm, he gently brushes back Freddy's hair from his forehead, and says, "I really squished ya."

Freddy, under the spell of the burglar brushing back his hair, says, as if in a dream, "It's all fine."

Feeling suddenly foolhardy in a surge of happiness closely related to what just happened, the burglar lifts Freddy up in the air with both arms, saying gleefully, "Look how light he is!"

Freddy, holding on tight around his neck, says, "Watch out that I don't fall."

The burglar shouts with joy, "Dat's not gonna happen!"

Freddy says: "By god, what are you doing…"

To Freddy's bewilderment, the burglar holds him in his arms, swinging him back and forth, laughing heartily and saying, "My little child!" And then he laughs out loud, turns beet red, no longer sees anything, hears anything, knows anything, and sings more than he speaks: "Now I'll pack ya off ta bed, lil child."

He then sets him down in bed: "Ya look real nice lyin' der."

Then he pauses, as if catching his breath, or trying to regain the upper hand.

Freddy, anticipating victory, says, "Now it's you who's trembling!"

The burglar, like Samson under Delilah's shears, replies, "I dunno…haf I ben drunk?"

Freddy, even more sure of victory: "What's wrong?"

The burglar replies: "I dunno…"

As if lost in thought, Freddy says, "You did squeeze me terribly hard."…

The burglar backs up a few steps out of embarrassment, "Why're ya lookin' at me like dat?"

"I'd say you're looking at me!"

"Omigod," the burglar says, "Is't hot in here."

And now begins a dialogue that is not attached to the words actually being spoken but like the nightingale's love song consists of only trills and tweets and warbles and sighs, and it starts over and over without becoming boring or becoming monotonous. It goes something like this:

"Yes," Freddy says, "terribly hot. Watch out…I'll open the window."—He starts to jump up to open it.

The burglar quickly bends over him, holding his arms down, "No, no…" (but no longer using a tone of command!)

Freddy says, softly, "Ah…now you're squeezing me again," and braces himself against him.

Turning him around, the burglar presses his head on Freddy's chest, causing his hat to fall off, and says, "Stay here."

"But my pajamas," says Freddy…

"So it'll tear," replies the burglar…

"But what are you doing?" says Freddy…

"Such white skin…so smooth…"

"You're biting me," says Freddy…

Then the burglar spreads out over him completely, saying, "You drive me mad!"

The clock on the mantel strikes 3:30 a.m.

The burglar rises with a start: "what?"

Freddy says, "What's wrong?"

"Is dat awready 3:30?"

"So what if it is.

"Omigod, I gotta go."

"Oh stay here," says Freddy.

"They'll catch me," says the burglar, but he makes no attempt to leave.

"Stay here," Freddy says, holding tight onto his arm, although that's no longer necessary.

The burglar strokes Freddy's hands, "so soft..."

Freddy pulls him back down. "Come here..."

Pressing against him passionately, the burglar says, "I could really squeeze you...You...you drive me mad..."

Freddy replies, "Ah, you...you..."

And with that, all words cease.

Until suddenly the burglar's conscience is aroused. He gets up and says, "I gotta go..."

Freddy, not paying much attention, says, "Hey, tell me your name.—I've no idea what your name is."

"My name's Shorgie...Call me Shorgie."—And then he laughs and says, "You can also call me Little Shorgie."

But then he pulls away and says, "Okay, now I gotta go!"

He gets up, straightens himself out, smoothing over his hair with the palm of his hand until it's neat again—for it had gotten messed up in the heat of passion—and then looks around for his things...

Suddenly he kneels down next to Freddy's bed and says, "You ain't mad at me?"

Freddy is at first surprised, then understanding. "No," he replies.

The burglar asks once again, even more intensely while grasping Freddy's hand, "Ya forgive me?"

And Freddy replies softly, "Yes."

"Ya know, I wont take nuttin' from ya," the burglar says, now almost pleading.

Freddy, who's utterly indifferent as to whether everything or nothing at all is taken from him, says only, "Okay."—For this could mean anything!

Yet Shorgie asserts one more time, "Im lettin' ya keep all your stuff."

Then hesitating and still a bit unsure of himself, he adds, "An I'll never do my nite work agin...I'll...Don't tink bad o' me..."— He can't find the right words, for he's like anyone who, having been derailed from their life's path by a sudden event, finds their customary way of living subverted, leaving them standing, so to speak, on the wreckage of their world view and feeling that they have to start all over again from the beginning to learn, to work, and to struggle.—Shorgie had really been something in his profession! At just twenty years old he'd already set several burglary records and was an accomplished thief. And now! What will happen with him now?—Oh uncertain future!

Freddy looks at him, who now kneels so quietly and questioningly next to him, also uncertain and questioning: "Do you really want to go?"

"I gotta go...Else Ill get caught..."—But then with sudden fervor says, "Ill see ya agin, eh?"

"Yes," says Freddy.

"When?"

"Tomorrow."

And all at once Shorgie passionately buries his lips one more time into Freddy's chest; then, pulling away from him, says, "I haf to see ya tomorrow!"

Freddy sits up, and reaching for him as if in a dream, says, "Yeah, sure..."

Then Shorgie takes a small green object from his pants pocket: "Here, take dis..."

"What is it?"

"My present to you," says Shorgie.

Genuinely surprised, Freddy says, "It's a scarab!"

"I dont know…but its sumtin' good."

Freddy then asks, inquisitorially, "Where'd you get it?"

Shorge replies matter of factly, "Some ol' guy, insanely rich, ya know!"

"Keep your stuff," Freddy says sternly."

But Shorgie insists, "Ya hafta keep it. Ya hafta promise me!"— And now slowly and simply: "And I promise you I wont do this no more. I promise."

Freddy shouts in a voice almost too loud for the late hour, "Shorgie, let's be friends."

Now the story begins to become a bit sentimental as Shorgie wipes his eyes.

Freddy, pretending not to see this, says, while looking over the stone, "This is really a genuine scarab…"

Shorgie also pretends that nothing had just happened and says, "There's a hole in it, 'cause it goes 'round yer nek."

And then, as Freddy still hesitates, Shorgie abruptly pulls him up to himself and says, squeezing him once more very firmly, "If ya dont wear it when I come to see ya moro nite…"

And lacking all willpower, Freddy says, "Yes, I'll be wearing it…Come about one o'clock."

"Okay…I gotta go now," says Shorgie. "God bless ya."

"Get home safe, Shorgie" says Freddy, as he starts to get up to see him to the door.

But Shorgie gently holds him back, "Stay, so ya dont catch cold…I'll find my way out…God bless ya Aalfreed."

"Alfred?"

"Yeah," dats wats in da drectry."

"Call me Freddy," he laughs, "that's my name."

"Okay, God bless ya, Freddy...moro nite, one o'clock!"—He takes his lantern and walks slowly toward the door without taking his eyes off Freddy, only to suddenly slide silently out of the room.

Freddy remains standing a few moments, listening carefully. He doesn't hear anything. Then he steps in front of the mirror, looks at himself, closes his eyes, leans his forehead against the glass, and smiles to himself. From the tray on the dressing table he picks up a very thin gold chain, threads it through the scarab, and hangs it around his neck.

Then he lights a cigarette and lies down on his bed.

Through the curtains, morning dawns.

AMERICAN STYLE

THE EXPRESS TRAIN FROM BOLOGNA TO MILAN HAS JUST PULLED into Ferrara on a beautiful, clear, breezy autumn day.

Franz Amhof has already taken his window seat. He's traveling first class because he's on a work trip, having served as a travel guide to Rome for a pack of art-loving young women, and so he doesn't worry about the expense, as he otherwise would have. The chattering geese just transferred to their connecting train, which is headed to Germany via the Brenner Pass. Now Franz, no longer wedded to his ladies and happy about his newfound freedom, is on the way back to his native Switzerland.

Franz Amhof studies art history in Bern, although he's neither as provincial nor as straightlaced as that city. If, like the medieval knights, he had a banner, its motto would be *Travel, Art, and Love!* Franz is a pleasant, amiable fellow, small rather than large, slim and wiry with sparkling eyes and a carefree expression.

Just before the train starts to move, a gentleman standing in the corridor sticks his head in, and, holding open the sliding door of the compartment, points to the empty seat opposite Franz to inquire with gestures and incomprehensible sounds, if the seat is free. Told that it is, he pushes two small, pristine leather suitcases into the compartment, swinging them up into the overhead net above the empty seat with a bold and practiced flair. But for all of his skill, he has the bad luck to have the train pull out with a mischievous lurch just as the second suitcase lands in place, causing him to lose his balance and end up with the full force of his personage in Franz Amhof's lap.

By way of apology, the man lets out a set of barely recognizable vowels, including e-a-o-u, in a nasal tone but which doesn't sound at all unfriendly. At this moment—truth be told!—Franz releases a subdued but rather high-pitched cry, prompting the gentleman to look around frantically to figure out whether he's sitting on a woman.

Now it's no trivial matter to suddenly have a man like this one sitting in your lap, for he's a very large, powerful person with mighty shoulders and iron limbs. A person whose imposing skull, moreover, seems carved in wood, and who is as beautiful and strong as Siegfried.

It also so happens that shortly before his trip to Italy, Franz Amhof had read Bernhard Kellermann's novel *The Tunnel*, and had thus formed a mental image of the enterprising, full-blooded American type: The iron will, practical sensibility, inexhaustible energy, vigorous constitution, and an inventiveness that promises unlimited possibilities. If Franz doesn't immediately discover all these virtues in his traveling companion, he's nonetheless certain even at first glance that he possesses them, just as he immediately knows that he's an American.

Soon thereafter the two men sit across from each other just like two well-bred worldly citizens. The train is running at full speed, and everything is in perfect order. For Franz, however, remaining in this middle-class order doesn't seem like the point of the journey, and so he silently begins to weave a plot.

He pulls a notebook from his bag and begins to search for a pencil in all the creases and folds of his suit. Just as he has brought the situation to the point where he can comfortably ask for a pencil from the person sitting opposite, the desired instrument is handed to him from there with the friendliest, if also incomprehensible, muttering.

Thus contact is established.

Franz scribbles down a few pro forma lines before returning the pencil, saying, "Thank you very much."

The American nods in a friendly manner and says, "Eaou!"

Franz now stumbles forth with his schoolboy knowledge of English: "Are you American?"

"Eaou yes!"…says the American, adding several more incomprehensible words. To which Franz, refusing to let this fragile hothouse blossom of a conversation wither away, replies: "Are you going to Milan?"

The American, who managed to understand the name of the city, says, "Milan!…eaou!"

Franz tries Italian, French, German—all in vain. And his English, too, has the misfortune of not being understood by the American. Despite that, they continue their conversation, conducting it, as it were, like a purely musical dialogue, where the sounds themselves, rather than the words, are the most critical factor. And in this way they gradually develop a mutual understanding.

On the surface, this is what happens:

First, they both admire the landscape, note that the train runs very quickly, and that the seats are very comfortable, among other innocent banalities. Then they step into the corridor to observe the landscape from the other side, but also so that the travelers who have since entered their compartment can't listen in on their conversation. After some misunderstanding, Franz figures out that the American has a connection of just several minutes in Milan before continuing on to Zurich.

The American asks repeatedly: "Are we going to be late?"

Franz assures him that the connecting train will wait for them. The American says "Yes," even though he doesn't understand what Franz said.

Then Franz gathers from what he says that he has some business in Zurich, that from there he needs to travel on to Paris immediately to buy a few automobiles, and that he then must return as quickly as possible to America.—Time is money!

Franz takes the liberty of asking, "What do you do for a living?" He thinks the American might be an engineer, inventor, or any of the unlimited possibilities of the protagonist in *The Tunnel*.

The American, shrugging his shoulders as if the answer were obvious, says, "I make buildings."

But Franz doesn't quite grasp his meaning, and says: "I study art...*les beaux arts*...history of art."

This time the American understands the words but doesn't see the purpose of what he says: "Art?...How much money do you make doing that?"

Franz evades this commonsense question by referring to his still unfinished course of study: "I'm still studying! I study!...I study!"

To which the American replies, "You need to learn how to make money!"

So, by all appearances, besides the difficulty in understanding each other, there now yawns a chasm between their different world views. It is clear their dialogue would certainly soon fade away if behind all the words there did not remain a certain unspoken something that stubbornly keeps the conversation chugging along.

And again it's the devious express train that pushes the plot of this hitherto perfectly ordinary comedy a bit forward, for just then, while rounding a sharp curve, it flings Franz forcefully against the window with the apparent goal of knocking him to the ground. Only the strong American arm prevents an accident, but the manner in which he grasps Franz makes it seem as though he intends to be something more than merely helpful. For a moment, the two travelers remain in a beautiful, enclosed heap. What reveals the thoughts and feelings of the American even further, however, is the sentence he utters shortly thereafter, which is understood by Franz more or less as follows: "You look just like a friend of mine!" This seems to Franz like a traditional expression of sympathy, although no less meaningful for that.

Franz reacts to this statement as if automatically with that sirenlike and cruel coquetry of certain feminine types who are being pursued and sure of their suitor. For just as the female pigeon first finds a thousand different ways to provoke, annoy, tease, and irritate the aroused male pigeon before she grants him any favors, just as she cannot perform enough ceremonial movements, sudden deflections, feigned pecking for food, or even intentions to fly away, so that she entangles the poor male pigeon ever deeper in his breast until he at last becomes her obedient slave, so, too, Franz plays the chaste, coy, innocent, yet ever more enticing seductress, so that the otherwise sensible American, for whom time is money, declares, shortly before arriving in Milan: "I'll stay the night in Milan if you do, too!"

Franz is both delighted and doubtful; he asks, "What hotel should we stay at?" The American says, "The Excelsior Palace, of course! Just as in Rome and Naples, these hotels are clean and comfortable."

Franz, hesitates for a moment, and then says, "I only go to budget hotels. I'm at the end of my trip and won't receive any more money until I get to Bern."—He thinks to himself: *If I'd not had my first-class ticket paid for by the travel group, I'd have gone third class. If I could only travel, see countries...!*—

But the American is prepared to sacrifice both his time and comfort: "We'll go together to a budget hotel then!" Consulting his Baedecker travel guide, the American downgrades to the Hotel du Nord. Franz knows the place. For someone in his circumstances, it's frightfully expensive. But whether for the sake of appearances or of adventure, he agrees.

In the lobby of the Hotel du Nord, the American registers his name: Mr. C. H. Bronklin, Chicago, U.S.A. Out of consideration for Franz, he asks for one room with two beds (since that's less expensive than two rooms with one bed each!).

Then they venture into the city, with Franz serving as guide. They go to the Vittorio Emanuele Gallery, the Cathedral, the Basilica of San Lorenzo, and the Castle, and even manage to work in Leonardo's *Last Supper*. Mr. C. H. Bronklin appreciates the practical appeal of the Gallery, the Cathedral, and the Castle; the painting speaks to him less. But while Franz works himself up into a frenzy struggling to explain the value of the artwork, the American suddenly says, "I don't know, I like you even better the longer we hang out!" With that, he casts an astonished look, now at Franz, now at the painting. And he even begins to find the painting beautiful, if not very practical.

As they step back outside, dusk arrives, which turns the streets more colorful and marvelous, prompting the American to say, "I've never seen such a beautiful evening!"

As they sit down to eat—Mr. Bronklin has invited Franz to a voluptuous dinner at the Gallery—he says, referring to Franz's homespun gray-green suit: "Your outfit has all the colors of the rainbow!" And later: "Your hands are so beautiful." And later still: "Your eyes are such an amazing blue!"—For on this day, a new world unfolded for this practical, prosaic American, who is used to seeing only the utility in things.

It's true that Franz has a hard time understanding everything the American says, but he knows exactly what is being said to him. He smiles like the Mona Lisa.

After dinner, they go to the opera: Donizetti's *The Elixir of Love*. Mr. C. H. Bronklin had never before in his life found time to go to the opera. After the first act, he asserts: "It's unnatural to sing one's actions; that doesn't happen in real life."

And Franz explains: "The dialogue is translated into an artificial realm, into music, whose truth doesn't lie in external form but in the inner expression of melody and rhythm." But he sets the subject of the dialogue too high for it to be comprehensible across the difference in language between them.

But then later Donizetti himself offers the proof. A small tenor, from whom one would not have expected much, sings the aria "Una furtiva lagrima." There radiates at once, with harmony and vocal beauty, a passionate, life-affirming sensation, casting a spell over the entire audience. It also sweeps up Mr. C. H. Bronklin from Chicago, making sport of all his practical precepts.

Until now the two have been sitting politely next to each other at a distance, but then the American puts his arm in Franz Amhof's arm. Later, on the street, they stroll arm in arm into the hotel and head directly up to bed.

The beds are far apart, each pushed chastely up against its own wall.

The light is turned off. Franz lies still with anticipation. The American tosses his pillow at him, prompting a pillow fight in the dark, until Franz finally thinks to himself: *Why continue with this foreplay?* He jumps over to Mr. Bronklin's bed and climbs under the covers without further ado.

Here the most extraordinary thing occurs which seems completely disconnected from anything the plot of this comedy has presented up to this point. It begins with the American saying, "But what are you doing?" And Franz, in the heat of the moment, slips into Swiss dialect: "It just feels so good..." The American, somewhat surprised, says, "Eaou...Now go to sleep."

Franz replies, "Oh, never mind...I'm just joking!"

Whereupon he simply kisses Mr. C. H. Bronklin on the lips, and then says: "I...I just like you so much."

Mr. C. H. Bronklin has grabbed both his arms and pushed him off to the side, saying, "We have to be sensible now and go to sleep...go back over to your bed!" Yet while saying this, his iron body trembles like a large ocean liner when the anchor cables rattle into the sea.

At this moment, Franz has a frightful scare. He thinks to himself: *Everything seemed to be going fine; first, his friendly manner, then his comparing me with his friend, the arrangement for the night, the shared hotel room, and then his wooing me, walking arm in arm...That's certainly everything you'd expect to find in a regular love affair!* Franz thinks further: *Heavens, how do I get myself out of this?*

But at the same time, he's also conscious of Mr. C. H. Bronklin's shaking.—And a breathless silence takes over the room.

Then and there Franz decides not to retreat but to fight, whatever the cost. He knows: Not raw power but the stronger will determines the victor.

He wrests himself away from Mr. Bronklin's grip and gives him another bold and unabashed kiss. Then he snuggles up to him, laughs, and whispers something, sliding his soft hands over the American forehead, the shoulders, the chest...

And the American, who has yet to recover from his surprise, sees, in spirit, him and Franz standing in front of Leonardo's painting, marvels at Franz's blue eyes sparkling from across the table in the Gallery, hears Donizetti's music, feels everywhere life, exhilaration, freedom…

The American keeps saying: "Don't do that…please, don't do that!" But only his mouth speaks these words, while his senses have long since given over to the magical arts of the wicked devil of love. But then, after all his protests have proven feckless, something surges within him. And just as if Niagara Falls had suddenly come over Chicago, so did passion now seize him with unbridled force.

Franz retreats to his own bed very late that night. The cleaning lady's knock on the door the following morning barely awakens him. Shortly afterward, however, Mr. Bronklin stands next to Franz's bed, bends down to him and says, half reproachfully and half apologetically, "We were so naughty last night! Such bad boys!"

And while Franz has not yet pulled himself together, Mr. Bronklin has already slipped into bed with him, and the nocturnal love duet begins all over again; only this time not modestly, in the dark, but rather freely and boldly in the bright morning light.

All of which goes to show that it was futile for the biblical God to have destroyed the Tower of Babel, distributing a cacophony of different languages among the peoples of the earth, for love has its own universally understood and universally powerful language.

At noon, Mr. C. H. Bronklin leaves for Zurich and Franz Amhof for Bern. Mr. Bronklin's train goes first.—The American leans out the window of the train while Franz stands on the platform. Both of them are very quiet, and both assume that they'll hardly see each other again. An ashen sadness fills each of them.

Suddenly the American says, "Don't think ill of me!" Franz blushes, feeling ashamed: "What will you think of me?" The

American goes to shake his hand: "I'm so happy that we got to meet. You've shown me that there's so much beauty in life." And as the train starts out, he shouts: "I never say 'good-bye,' I always say 'till I see you again.'"

Nearly a year later, the one piece of news that Franz Amhof received from the American from Chicago contained the following message: "Mr. and Mrs. C. H. Bronklin humbly announce their matrimony."

CADETS

THE MAIN CADET ACADEMY IN GROSS-LICHTERFELDE, NEAR Berlin. Eighth Company, Barrack 9.—Along the gray walls, nine uniformly spaced lockers, each crowned with a row of blue-covered textbooks. Above them, several paintings of emperors and battle scenes, and a pendulum clock. In the middle of the room, two large, square tables with four chairs each. Between the windows, a smaller, separate table for the room's eldest cadet. The furniture is painted in a functional, loveless brown. On the windows, gray linen curtains that can be drawn shut.

A summer evening. Outside it's seductively beautiful; in the barracks, stuffy and hot.

Seven cadets sit on their chairs busily reading, writing letters, and sewing on buttons. The room's eldest, Sergeant von Rimpau, an eighteen-year-old of medium height with an attractive, youthful face, strolls about; he looks over the shoulders of some of his subordinates to see what they're reading, and then checks whether a button that cadet Lange had just sewn on is tight enough, finally succeeding, after much twisting and pulling, in tearing it off, whereupon he orders the cadet to report to detention for shoddy button sewing.

He then turns to the corner shelf where the water bottle sits; he shouts, "Clean-up crew!" Cadet von Schmidt jumps to his feet: "Here!" The room's eldest says, "Did you fetch fresh water before the recess period?" Cadet von Schmidt begins to reply "No, Sir, I was going to…" before Sergeant von Rimpau cuts him off:

"Detention!" "At your command!" Cadet von Schmidt replies.

Sergeant von Rimpau goes to the next "cell." After a while, he shouts: "Clean-up crew!" Cadet von Schmidt says "Here!" and runs into the room. Sergeant von Rimpau asks, "Why isn't the bootjack under the washstand?" Cadet von Schmidt falls silent. "Tomorrow and the next day you'll also report to detention," says the Sergeant. "At your command!" says Schmidt.

Meanwhile, in the barracks, cadets Englert and Graf Boser are quietly talking.—Rimpau returns immediately: "Who's been talking here?" No one replies. "I've forbidden anyone to talk during recess. Now I'm asking, who's been talking?" Still no reply. Rimpau says, "From now on, till further notice, the entire barracks will step into formation for roll call fifteen minutes early and stand still in the hallway."

Cadet von Alberti steps into the room from the hallway, saying "Here!" Rimpau: "Where have you been?" Alberti hesitates a moment, but before he can reply, Rimpau says quickly, "Report to detention!" "At your command," says Alberti.—He goes to his spot and takes a book out of his drawer to read, or at least pretends to be reading.—Cadet von Alberti is not very tall, with very slim hips and slender, delicate limbs. His face is almost pale. Dark circles form under his deep brown eyes, and his head is always bent forward a bit; overall, there is something unmilitary-like in his bearing.

Sergeant von Rimpau heads over to his own spot, also picks up a book, and from there keeps a close watch on Cadet Alberti.—All that can be heard are the ticking of the clock and the scratching sound from the pen of Cadet Fritz Rieper, who's writing a letter.

Then the shrill electric bells ring out in the hallway. Nine thirty. Recess is over.

Cadets Lange, Schmidt, and Alberti immediately prepare for

detention, gathering their field uniforms, helmets, sword belts, bayonets, and ammunition pouches. They need to finish cleaning everything by 9:45. The other cadets use the fifteen minutes of free time to talk to friends in the hallway. At five minutes before ten, everyone—except for those in detention—has to be in bed.

Sergeant Schäfer from Barrack 13 comes over to Barrack 9.— He's blond and tall, almost stately; on his upper lip the first wisps of a beard begin to show.—Dispensing with the other cadets with an incidental "evening," he approaches Rimpau and says, "Hello, Rimpau...Well...?" Rimpau looks at him for a moment, the corner of his mouth quivering slightly, and says, "What do you actually want around here?" Schäfer has a guilty conscience. And he's too honorable to create some sort of scene right now. He just says, "Just don't be like that again!" Rimpau says very quietly, in a tone intended to sound as indifferent as possible, "At the very least, you don't need to keep him away during recess." Schäfer looks over at Alberti, who's blushing, and who, to prevent others from seeing, bends over as far as possible while polishing his buttons.

Finally, Schäfer says to Rimpau (quietly, so as not to diminish his authority): "Man, are you ever an old stickler!" To which Rimpau replies, now with an edge to his voice, "I suppose I should send your tricks over there myself!" Schäfer says, impatiently, "Oh, he's not my trick!" Rimpau says bitterly, his voice quietly quivering, "So...? What is he then...?"

Schäfer finds himself in a tight spot, "God knows I like him a lot...That's all!"—Then he wants to cut the Gordian knot with his sword. Taking Rimpau abruptly by the arm, he pulls him away and says, "Come on, Rimpie, let's go to the hallway for a bit." Rimpau pulls away from him and says, "No, I still have a few cadets in detention...Anyway, I have a stomachache." Schäfer shrugs his shoulders: "Okay, if you don't want to. But I'm telling you, God knows you don't need to bother yourself with this…!"— He then takes hold of Sergeant Rimpau's neck with his right hand and with his left gently pats his cheek. For the benefit of the three subordinates present, Rimpau frees himself forcefully, saying, "You're crazy!"—Inside, however, he feels something very much like satisfaction. Schäfer then leaves the barrack whistling the Torgau March, not deeming the other cadets worthy of any further greeting.—

At detention, cadets Lange, Schmidt, and Alberti have to unfasten their field uniforms to show the linings.—As Rimpau inspects Alberti's lining, their eyes meet by chance. Both get a scare. Both are thinking at this moment of the same thing. Finally, Rimpau plucks at Alberti's lining mechanically as though he were scrutinizing it, but in reality he's thinking about Schäfer.—

Suddenly he says, "Schmidt, fall out!…Forward, clean up the room! Lange, you too, fall out! Go at once to room four and tell Sergeant von Redern to lend me his math book." And after Schmidt has disappeared into the room and Lange has gone out into the hallway, he pulls Alberti up close by his collar and asks, at last, very quietly but without mincing words, "Why are you taking my friend away from me?"

Alberti is silent.

Rimpau, now more plainly, says, "Do you think I don't see what's going on?…Do you think I don't know that you've been getting up and leaving every night,…and where to?…Answer me!"

Alberti remains silent.

Rimpau, softly but urgently, says, "You'll answer me!" "Yes sir, Sergeant!" Alberti replies.

Whether non-commissioned Sergeant von Rimpau now feels

he would relinquish his authority by conducting this kind of intimate conversation with a subordinate, or whether he is overcome by an (oh!) all-too-human feeling of jealousy,—he, who otherwise always holds up his severity, at whose nod of the head eight submissive cadets just flew into every corner of the academy, who lorded it over his barrack like Napoleon did over the world, he, the upperclassman, in negotiating with a small underclassman over the story of an affair, now becomes uncertain, timid, and vulnerable!—He plays with the shiny buttons of Alberti's field uniform, looks down at his boots, now polished to a high-gloss, flawless black, and says, "No, you need to tell me truthfully just what's going on...I won't do anything to you. Look, I could simply work you until you sweat blood, but I have no intention at all of doing that...On the contrary, I've treated you quite decently...haven't I?"

Alberti wishes at this moment he were anywhere else in the world. He replies softly, "Yes, sir!" While keeping his hand on Alberti's shoulder, Rimpau asks, "Okay? What's going on...?"

Rimpau stands and waits. He can't issue an order for Alberti to answer him. Out of embarrassment, he keeps twisting Alberti's buttons, as is his habit but now until they nearly fall off. He then says softly, "You see, the bike race is coming up soon, in which he and I ride together as part of a group, and then there'll be summer vacation, which he's supposed to spend on our estate. Last winter we'd already thought about what it would be like. Mornings we'd go for a ride, then swimming in the Weser River. Or we'd do a day-long hike and just sleep in the fields ....You know, I've been looking forward to this vacation in the craziest way!...Oh, but this summer will be nothing compared to what we've planned for later. We've mapped out our entire life together. When we get out of military school, then things will really fall into place. We'll be together forever, we'll enlist in the same regiment...We want to really support each other's ambitions..."

He breaks off, his heart pounding, waiting anxiously to hear what Alberti has to say.

Alberti looks at the room's eldest.—At this moment an intangible bridge forms between the two of them; an animating warmth suffuses the cold militarism.—After a few moments, Alberti replies (without of course violating the prescribed language of subordination), "Sergeant, sir, believe me, I'm not Sergeant Schäfer's trick...even if once I've been together in that way with Sergeant Schäfer." And Alberti swears to himself not to have anything more to do with Schäfer, and even to say to Schäfer that he shouldn't neglect Rimpau, and that he himself would retreat...

Rimpau says, "If you...do something once in a while with Sergeant Schäfer, it's all the same to me, but..."—And then he shrugs his shoulders, not knowing how to express himself, when suddenly he snaps like a pocketknife and presses his hands against his stomach, "Oh, hell no! This damn stomachache!"

Alberti would like to demonstrate some goodwill toward him to show he's sincere. He asks, "Can I perhaps help you somehow, Sergeant?"

At that moment the other cadets are noisily returning to the barrack. Now the human has to fall silent and the cadet must reappear!...

Like Jupiter, who seizes his lightning bolt to stir up a storm, Rimpau transforms his vulnerability into the severest authoritative tone, shouting into the room, "Straight to bed! Everyone needs to be in bed by the time I count to three!...Clean-up crew! The inkstands are still on the tables. They're gonna be out there all night? Damn deadbeats!...——"

Alberti seizes an opportunity to slip out into the hallway for a second. Schäfer's there, as if by chance, of course. Alberti whispers quickly, "I can't see you tonight...I'll explain everything tomorrow!" Schäfer, taken aback, says, "Hey, what's going on?" "It has to do with Sergeant Rimpau." Schäfer replies, "Oh, he won't notice anything. Of course you're coming!...If you don't come, I'll come to you!"

The conversation is cut short by Sergeant von Bennecke, who suddenly sticks his head out of room 8 to yell: "Apparently someone likes to take a walk with his tricks in the hallways every evening at ten." At that, Alberti slips as quickly as possible back into his room while Schäfer, whistling the Torgau March, and with a hand in his pocket, strolls nonchalantly into Barrack 13.

At 11 p.m. the officer on duty retires from his post. Schäfer waits until about 11:30...But when Alberti still hasn't arrived, he gets up quietly, carefully opens the door to the hallway, and listens a bit longer; he then sneaks down the dark hallway like a ghostly sleepwalker until he gets to the door of room 9, where he stands still, listening; he quietly presses the latch down and opens the door just a bit, when its creaking sound startles Schäfer. As he carefully pushes the door farther, it creaks some more, frustrating Schäfer to the point he'd just like to kick it open. But reason prevails, and after listening for a few moments longer, he opens the door wider. It keeps creaking as if it had a mind of its own. Schäfer forges ahead, braving the danger. He can now slip in through the opened door.—When he's finally inside the room, he carefully closes the door behind him, which now emits just a slight moan.

Inside the room, only the breathing sounds of the sleepers can be heard, and from down the hall the ticking of the clock. The small little lamp on the corner shelf gives off a modest, faint light. Schäfer sneaks up to Alberti's bed, which is placed in the corner, just to the right of the door, and thus has only one other bed on one side. That's actually a good thing because all the other beds are next to each other in the room, with only a small bit of space between them, as if arranged in formation.

Schäfer bends over close to Alberti and touches him softly on the shoulder, whispering, "Hey...!" Alberti mutters something, clicks his tongue a few times as if he were tasting something, and then continues sleeping calmly. In order not to just stand there leaving himself exposed, Schäfer quickly slips in under Alberti's covers, puts his arms around him and kisses him on the mouth. That wakes up Alberti, who opens his eyes wide for a few seconds before breaking out into a sweet smile.—He whispers, "It's you...!" Schäfer replies in hushed tones (so softly that the many hard German consonants can't even be noticed), "My dear boy...What got into you tonight?" Alberti frowns, "Oh, yeah...! You know...We have to stop seeing each other. I don't wanna hurt anybody." Schäfer pulls him up close to himself, "But what's up with you all of a sudden!..."

Alberti insists, "He talked to me tonight...Not in an official way! If he'd given me an official order, I wouldn't care. But he told me just as a friend that he knew everything..."

Schäfer says, "Oh, I'll see him tomorrow about it. He and I will stay friends. I like him a whole lot too, just not as much as before...It's just that I'm in love with you! Is that my fault?"

And then, he wraps his strong arms tight around Alberti's trembling body, grasps his pale, delicate, youthful head with both hands, and smothers his lips with kisses. Alberti loses his senses, and along with them, his good intentions. After all, it's the nights spent with Schäfer that have just now awakened this sixteen-year-old to life!

All at once something in the other corner of the room can

be heard, from the bed of the room's eldest. It's the sound of a soft, long-drawn-out breath, like a groan. Then a figure gets up and wanders along the row of beds and goes into the room to the corner shelf, where he pours himself some water and quickly drinks it.—Finally the figure returns to his bed by the same route and lies back down.

During all this, Schäfer and Alberti lie stone-still, except for the pounding of their hearts, which seems to create an actual, audible sound. For a long time after Rimpau lies back down they don't dare move because Rimpau seems to be moaning softly. At last, after things become completely silent again, Schäfer crawls out of bed and sneaks away. He moves so quietly that one hears only the cracking of his ankles. In order to avoid the creaky door, he heads for another door leading to the hallway.—But just as he reaches that door, Rimpau suddenly sits straight up in his bed and stares at him. Schäfer escapes. He slams the door of the room in such a panic that a loud echo fills the long hallway. Schäfer runs down the hall before disappearing into Barrack 13.

The next morning, immediately after breakfast, Rimpau reports to the infirmary. He can barely stand up from the pain. Like every-one who reports sick, he first has his temperature taken. He has a fever of over 102 degrees and is moved at once to the hospital.

Barrack 9 is thus liberated from tyranny.

Englert says, "If he gets over his stomachache, maybe he'll be in a better mood and stop mistreating us." Graf Boser laughs, "Now you see what comes of being a trick; he's having a baby!—"

At evening roll call the company officer on duty informs the cadets that Sergeant von Rimpau has taken a turn for the worse and that his mother has already been telegraphed. The bicycle race scheduled for tomorrow will be postponed for the time being. The next morning, Sergeant von Rimpau dies in the hospital.— That evening, Schäfer and Alberti stand next to each other behind the screen door of the hallway. They avoid each other's eyes, instead staring at the ground. Finally Schäfer shrugs his shoulders and says, "It's not something one could have known about." "No, I had no idea either, says Alberti. "He was thoroughly decent," says Schäfer. Alberti says, "I was in a room with him for such a long time, but I only really got to know him the day before yesterday, when he told me about his plans for summer vacation. At that point I suddenly liked him…"

Schäfer says, "I think I'd been mean to him in his last weeks." Alberti says, "If I could have only talked to him yesterday!…" Schäfer: "Yes, I wanted to tell him everything yesterday, too…" Alberti: "Now he thinks…" "Yeah, now it's too late," says Schäfer.

The bugler plays taps in the courtyard. It's already the second time. Schäfer and Alberti quickly split up, each running back to his barrack.—

On the third day, there is a funeral service for non-commissioned Sergeant von Rimpau. First in the chapel, then, led by the cadet band, in a procession to the train station, from where the body will be transported to his hometown.—On top of the coffin sits the small cadet helmet with a black plume. The entire cadet corps follows the coffin.

The band plays the Funeral March from Beethoven's *Eroica*.—A rather unmilitary-like tear rolls down Alberti's face; one after the other…

APPARITION

THE MAIN STREET OF SAINT-DENIS, A SUBURB OF PARIS.

The street runs almost directly from the train station up to the grand old cathedral, whose gigantic façade overlooks the town. The street is rather narrow; the houses are tall, consisting of several stories and long, gallery-like balconies. After several unpleasant rainy days, suddenly clear, bracing, autumn weather has returned, with white, wispy clouds dotting a magnificent blue sky. Actually, it's more like a summer day that has gotten lost! It's Sunday afternoon and everyone in Saint-Denis is out in the street. Musicians, balladeers, acrobats, magicians…All the swarming multitudes of factory workers roaming about in their holiday get-up.

Reinhard Dieffenbach has been in the cathedral visiting the tombs of the French kings. Still completely under the spell of the age-old stained-glass windows, he goes, detached from the world, as it were, through the noisy streets, intending to catch the next train back to Paris.—

Reinhard Dieffenbach has already reached that age where no one asks any longer how old you are. Should someone inquire about it, he'd answer today just as he did six years ago, with equanimity, politeness, and a touch of irony, 29!—One could, moreover, take him for that!

As the family of Reinhard Dieffenbach (or, in fact, *von* Dieffenbach!) says, as do his former classmates and army buddies, who in the meantime have all raised families and entered into civil service, indeed, as everyone says who knew him before,

Reinhard Dieffenbach has gone around the bend. First he studied law because that was the family tradition; then, when that was too dull and sober and mundane for him, he studied art, and studied and studied...until one day he got unlucky, and the police got involved in his misfortune...Well, and then the family simply didn't want him in Germany anymore.—He's now been employed for three years at Poiret, the Paris fashion house, as "Chef de Reception." There, he converses with the customers not only in French but also, as the need arises, in German and English, and, when the magic of fashion unfolds on the runway, assumes the role of artistic interpreter.—He has a small apartment in the Rue des deux Ponts, on the old island of Paris, travels twice daily on the Métro to work and back, and eats twice a day for one and a half francs at Chartier. Living in Paris, which is so beautifully foreign and with no memories of the past, has brought him an entirely new life. He has no more affairs and therefore no more sorrow. He's buried all his passions and become wonderfully superficial; there's no longer anything that could derail him. He's happy when he sees a beautiful face, he enjoys a good time, but he no longer gives over his lifeblood to it. He's achieved distance from life and become wise.—

When Reinhard Dieffenbach has walked down the street a short way, someone from behind suddenly grabs hold of his left arm. He looks back quickly and stands still in astonishment, not knowing right off what it means. On his arm hangs a young apache[1] who, looking directly at him and showing his white teeth along with a

---

1 This word was first used by a Parisian journalist to refer to young men from poor backgrounds in street gangs known for violence, a disregard for authority, and their flashy style. However inaccurate and insulting to Indigenous Americans whose resistance against the U.S. government was widely reported in Europe only decades earlier, the term was later adopted by artists and others to express a stylized defiance of convention.

mischievous smile, says, "Je v' d'mande pardon, 'sieur..."

In moments of our lives when a singular occurrence abruptly assails us, a bewildering thought process starts working that brings everything else to the surface except the very presence of mind or mastery of the situation required, and just as in such moments it is as though a film filled with memories whirrs away frantically inside us, so the sight of the apache youth revives in Reinhard Dieffenbach all the apache stories he has heard.

To begin with, there's the incident that Emil Grillon recounted. One time, in broad daylight, on a small street in the Latin Quarter, near Boule Michel, he was asked by a man for the time of day. And as he pulls his watch from his pocket, suddenly there's a second man, and Emil is looking at a pistol right in front of his nose, and he is calmly robbed of all of his possessions while the sounds of the safe boulevard continue to ring mockingly from only steps away.

And the story Guillaume Racontin tells, who lives near Reinhard in the rue des deux Ponts, about exiting the Métro one night at the St. Paul station (it was the last run of the evening) and a young girl asks him if he would just walk with her to the next corner building, down the small side street that branches off from the rue Rivoli right by the station, and he came within a hair of being mugged by a gang of apaches—had he not recognized the ruse at the last moment and sprinted like a madman back to the main street.

And finally, even what happened to himself one night in the Bois de Boulogne!—There, because it was a beautiful evening, he had turned down a dark side path away from the well-lighted avenue; he was at first completely alone, when he heard someone near him to the right—walking at a distance of about ten steps from him, in the bushes, keeping the same pace as he. Then someone else approached, but right after passing him turned around to follow him. Suddenly someone else in front of him was going in the same direction as he, and, lest any direction be left out, someone else can be seen to the left of him in the bushes. But even more remarkable was that, as he suddenly reversed course because he started to feel uneasy, all the others likewise turned around to follow him. Then and there he came to the inevitable conclusion that he'd be caught like a mouse in a trap, and for sure in an instant one of them would commit that crime that occurs so frequently in Paris at night.

He recalls how, in his fear, he hit on the idea to start singing a racy song in a loud and boorish way. And how he eventually heard a whistle coming from the bushes, an extremely faint whistle, which, however, by its sound, gets your attention, giving you goose bumps; a whistle that started out very low, increased gradually like a foghorn to a shrill pitch and ended back in a low vocal range. Shortly thereafter, all those figures around him disappeared in a flash, the path lay free in front of him; the world opened up for him again and, his heart beating fast, he resumed his walk along the well-lighted avenue, where proper, carefree people were promenading up and down, just like always...—

Reinhard Dieffenbach stares at the apache youth next to him. The lad is no taller than he, has a youthful, round, fresh-looking face with coal-black eyes and thick black eyebrows. Under a small, daring nose smiles a half-open mouth with full, sensual lips. A large, black newsboy cap is pulled down on his forehead, which, however, doesn't keep a strand of blue-black hair, as if out of sheer insolence, from wriggling its way far down along the left side of his face. He's wearing a black linen outfit; a tight, fitted jacket reaching just to the hips and buttoned in front, and his trousers, extremely wide at the hips, are tapered at the ankles.

The get-up is topped off by a loud red tie and a wool scarf in the same shade of red, slung around his waist and sticking out from under the short jacket.

Reinhard tries to keep going, but the apache grabs hold of Reinhard's arm as if to prevent him from moving on, and says, "Don't worry...I'm a friend!" And because Reinhard just continues to keep going, carrying the apache along with him, the youth repeats, "You needn't worry. I'm a friend, you understand?...Really!"

But Reinhard is not only having visions of all his apache stories, he's also picturing to himself how this moment must look to everyone on this pedestrian-clogged main street of Saint-Denis. He thinks how improbable it must seem for him, who after all is dressed like he belongs to the top ten percent, to be walking down the sidewalk arm in arm with a young apache. He imagines that a crowd of people would form on the spot, that the whole world would be laughing...

He says, "I don't understand you!" The apache keeps saying, "Come on, just say it!...You're afraid. But you shouldn't be, because you'll see that I'll be your friend." Reinhard replies, even more emphatically, while trying (in vain) to free himself from the youth, "I don't understand you!" The apache, although not letting go, is momentarily at a loss. Shrugging his shoulders, he says, "How should I say...Je n' parl' pas i-ingli-ish ...." And then, after hesitating briefly, says, "Okay, then. Do you trust me?...Do you want to come with me?" Reinhard, still obsessed with what other people on the street might think, finally says, "I don't have time, I need to catch a train."

At this point the apache, who up to now had allowed himself to be dragged along, blocks his way, "All right. You don't want to! You don't trust me!...Give me your hand!"—With that he lets go of Reinhard and extends his right hand, his Sunday-scrubbed hand that is immaculately clean except for those tiny creases, deep down, tinged by that dark patina of factory work that no soap can expunge.

Reinhard cautiously takes hold of the extended hand. The apache squeezes Reinhard's hand passionately, and looks directly and openly into his eyes, "All right, if you don't want to…if you really don't want to…then…adieu!" He then runs diagonally across the street and disappears.

Reinhard looks around self-consciously; had someone been watching him?—But the people on the street are all preoccupied with their own affairs, with their children, their neighbors, the street performers. Not even a cat was paying any attention to him. Nevertheless, Reinhard wants to get out of this place as quickly as he can. At the station he finds a commuter train right away that's headed for Paris and takes a seat in a third-class coach.

Yet scarcely has the train put some distance between himself and Saint-Denis that regret sneaks up on Reinhard.—He thinks, *Ah, this apache was different from the kind you usually meet…And he gave me such a peculiar look…and God knows!…the guy had style! There was really something about him…*

And he itches to get off at the very next stop and walk down the street in Saint-Denis one more time. But the train would have nothing of it. It doesn't just stop when a passenger feels like getting off, being a punctilious, reliable commuter train without local stops.

Thus Reinhard quickly ends up back in Paris.

That evening he talks with Guillaume Racontin about what happened. Racontin finally says, "Man, you were such an idiot!" He also compliments him: "When you take such good care of yourself, why wouldn't a young apache be attracted to you!"

The following Sunday Reinhard returns to Saint-Denis. He walks down the main street from the train station to the cathedral and back again, then does it one more time. There are a thousand apaches around. As if waiting to be chosen! But not the one he's looking for. At times, Reinhard thinks he's spotted him, causing him to feel a jolt, but on each occasion he's wrong.—Besides, it's a gray day, the houses are grimy, the people's faces grim,—all of life is stupid! Reinhard ventures once more into the street, lingering at that place where the apache met up with him. It is getting dark, outside on the street and within him. Finally, he realizes that there's no reason to keep standing around, so he returns to Paris. There, he walks along the grand boulevards. But even the boulevards, with their many lights and crowds of people, seem cheerless today.—He finally walks home, to the Rue des deux Ponts, hoping to run into Racontin, but he's gone out. Alone, Reinhard stands in his room. He's lit all the lights in his room, but they can't extinguish the darkness.

Finally, he goes out to the Café du Panthéon, sits at a table and orders a grenadine. The café is teeming with people. The orchestra plays "Louise" by Charpentier. Young ladies with pretty, made-up faces parade among the tables. The bustling atmosphere of café life does him some good for the moment.

A lovely young blonde approaches Reinhard's table, graciously takes hold of the vacant chair and says, "With your permission, Monsieur?" Reinhard is startled, as if who knows what could happen. He stammers, "Pardon!…The seat is taken…I'm waiting for someone." Smiling, Mademoiselle nods her head, "For a little lady?" Rising from his seat, Reinhard bows, as if at the royal court's annual ball, saying, "But yes…Of course!" The girl gives him a friendly nod: "All right, then…Bonsoir, monsieur." Once she's gone, Reinhard thinks to himself, *Why didn't I invite her to have a grenadine, at least then I wouldn't be sitting alone.*

Shortly afterward, Emile Grillon arrives at the café. Reinhard waves him over and says, "How swell that we should meet here!" Grillon sits down with him and says, "I don't see you around anymore…And you don't even know what's been going on…" Sitting back in his chair, he crosses his legs and blows smoke from his cigarette up to the ceiling of the café, as if he were the grand mogul. Then he says, "I'm getting married! Marion and I, we are about to tie the knot! We had our fill of the highlife and want to become regular citizens. She'll be here soon, in fact."—And then he hums along with the waltz that the orchestra has begun playing.

Suddenly, with a gleam in his eyes, he bends over closely to Reinhard and says, "If I ask you to be the godfather…would you do it?" Reinhard looks at him, amazed. Grillon says, "Well, just between us…in four or five months!"—He then resumes his humming, even swinging along in his seat to the tune of the waltz. Reinhard puts on a happy face and says, "But of course!"—And silently he thinks, *You lucky one!*

Soon Marion arrives.—She glides, all ladylike elegance, first to Reinhard, "Oh, monsieur Die-ffen-bac…!" Grillon has already gotten her a chair. Then he says, "Yes, my little Marion, here's where we first met one year ago. Do you remember?…Now let's toast to the good old Café du Panthéon."—And he gently strokes her hand resting on the table as she smiles up at him. Then he orders wine. Later he says, "It's so good when you know exactly what kind of woman you're marrying; then you won't be disappointed after the wedding." All three drink to that.

Finally Emile Grillon heads home with his lady friend. Reinhard stays behind alone, more alone than ever.

The poor wise man! He had believed himself to stand above and apart from life and now he sees how easily all worldly wisdom can just go to the devil if only a bit of lifeblood keeps coursing through your veins.—He can no longer ride the Métro without imagining a certain dark apache youth sitting next to him. He no longer eats at Chartier without secretly looking around for him. Every day he waits impatiently for work to be over and every evening is disappointed by the emptiness of his free hours.

And very soon it's no longer the dark apache that he looks for, but the other "I," the *one* person he can live for and who belongs to him. Yes, the incident in Saint-Denis, after it's in reality already over, begins only now to become truly real for him, for it's gone far beyond the mere incident and opens infinite perspectives. It's no use for Reinhard to fight against it by telling himself, *How ridiculous to dwell on such a thing just because it has the fascination of the unfulfilled. How stupid to take seriously what in the end is just a minor Parisian adventure, and in the suburbs to boot!*

That, however, is abstract knowledge; life doesn't know anything about that.

And so the incident in Saint-Denis brings the entire structure of his life crashing down, which he'd so painstakingly constructed. It shows him that he'd deceived only himself with it.—It says: your daily bread nourishes only your body. The little bit of elegance in your life is a sham. Paris—with its theaters, its parties, with all its glittering adventures—is a swindle. Your move to another country is only an escape from yourself. You run from yourself because you're afraid of your true self, which is boundlessly sad. And you believed yourself to be wise and able to renounce love, which is after all the center of all life. To be sure, your love, too, is a delusion. For always, when you love, it's just an episode; you don't ever love like Emile Grillon loves, with the certainty of a future... The only thing that's true is that you are and will remain alone.—

And he sees the experience in Saint-Denis as the apparition of a happiness that life denies him.

AFTERWORD
by Manfred Herzer

IN JUNE 1939 A COMMEMORATIVE EXHIBITION WAS ORGANIZED in Rio de Janeiro for the painter, writer and theater director Erwin Ritter von Busse, who had died shortly before, on April 10th, in São Paulo. On this occasion, the gallery owner Theodor Heuberger published a small catalog containing reproductions of several paintings by Busse, two shorter prose texts ("Impressions of Brazil"), a directory of his artistic oeuvre and a brief biography.[1] This text is the most substantial and currently known source about von Busse's life. What goes unmentioned, however, is the fact that he published two novella collections, *Das erotische Komödiengärtlein* [*Erotic Comedy Garden*][2] and *Liebesmärchen* [*Lovers' Fairy Tales*],[3] under the pseudonym Granand in 1920 and 1921.

---

1 Memorial Exhibition Dr. E. von Busse-Granand. Galerie Heuberger. Rio de Janeiro, Rua Buenos Aires, 79, June 29 to July 19, 1939. São Paulo, Rua Barão de Itapetininga, 41; also. July 31 to August 19, 1939. (The Ibero-American Institute at the Free University in Berlin owns one edition of the catalogue.) The catalogue also contains the only known portrait of Busse, which is the reproduction of a painting by the London painter Charles Horsfall.

2 The first edition was printed privately in 1920, with drawings by Rudolf Pütz.-Granand: *Das erotische Komödiengärtlein*. Zeichnungen von Ludwig Kainer, (First edition; Berlin: Almanach-Verlag, 1920).

3 *Lovers' Fairy Tales*. Retold by Granand. Drawings by Ludwig Kainer (Berlin: Almanach-Verlag, 1921).

Granand is identified as Erwin Ritter von Busse in several directories from the twenties, and by 1925 at the latest he himself added the pseudonym to his real name and started to call himself Erwin von Busse-Granand.

Clear proof of his authorship of the *Erotic Comedy Garden* is provided in a letter of February 19, 1921, held today in the theater museum of the University of Cologne; in it von Busse wrote to the Germanist Max Martersteig from Munich, among other things: "I would like to ask you about the book I wrote under my author's pseudonym Granand, against which the accusation of indecency has been raised, and that I am sending along so that you may provide me your assessment of the indecency charge."[4] The two editions of *Erotic Comedy Garden* had in fact been suppressed in two separate decisions of courts in Berlin and Leipzig, in 1920 and 1921. According to § 41 of the German Criminal Code, all editions consequently had to be confiscated and "made unusable." The public prosecutor's office had sought but failed to reach a similar ruling against Granand's more harmless and strictly "heterosexual" *Lovers' Fairy Tales,* which are literary imitations of selections from Washington Irving's *Tales of the Alhambra.* As a result of these rulings passed so soon after publication, the *Erotic Comedy Garden* was hardly reviewed or acknowledged at the time. It was not until 1938 that a reprint of the novella "The Apparition" appeared in *Menschenrecht* [Human Right], a gay magazine from Zurich, and since then there have been partial reprints in various gay magazines.

The little that we know today about the author of the *Erotic Comedy Garden* is easy to report: He was born on January 12, 1885 in Magdeburg as the first son of a Prussian officer family, attended schools in Magdeburg and Kiel and was enrolled from 1898 in

---

4   Polunbi-catalogue (Berlin 1926) 109.

various military academies (secondary schools), including in Gross-Lichterfelde near Berlin, where he earned the high school baccalaureate in 1905. After two years of service in the army, he began to study law in Munich in 1907, which he abandoned in 1909 to study art history. In 1912 he interrupted his studies to take part in an months-long expedition to Brazil, his future home, and stayed in Paris for some time. In the same year he resumed his studies at the University of Bern, where he received his doctorate in art history in 1914.[5]

From Bern, Busse then seems to have moved directly to Berlin. We find him listed in the Berlin directory of 1917 as "director and dramaturge at the Deutsches Theater", and there is evidence from the years 1918 and 1919 that he directed at least three chamber productions at the Deutsches Theater.[6] In the following year Busse moved from Berlin to Munich, where he seems to have entered the most creative phase of his life. He wrote not only his two literary works, but also continued the directorial work that he had begun under Max Reinhardt in Berlin at the Munich Schauspielhaus, which was then led by Hermine Körner. In 1921, von Busse was the director for at least two productions: George Bernard Shaw's *Candida* with Hermine Körner in the title role, and Jakob Lenz's *The Soldiers*.

Erwin von Busse ended his activity at the theater around 1923; in the "German Stage Yearbook" of 1925 he is mentioned without being assigned to a specific theater, and from 1926 onwards he no longer appears at all in the membership directory of the Stage Members' Cooperative.

As the fourth and final of his publications, apart from his

---

5   Erwin Ritter von Busse, *The Historical Evolution of Depictions of the Masses in Italian Painting*. Dissertation submitted at the University of Bern (Munich: Beck, 1914).

6   See Heinrich Huesmann, *World Theater Reinhardt* (Munich: Prestel, 1983).

dissertation, the *Erotic Comedy Garden* and the *Lovers' Fairy Tales*, in 1925 he published an 18-page essay on the Venetian painter Francesco Guardi, which includes a selection of 20 reproductions of Guardi's images.[7] Then, we must assume, his literary muse fell silent, and there seems to have been a break in his life in several respects: He converted to Catholicism, he married in London on April 10, 1933, when he was almost fifty years of age, and he emigrated to Brazil. [8]

We do not know the exact date of von Busse's departure from Europe for Brazil. One of his texts in the exhibition catalog is dated "Rio de Janeiro, May 1928," but according to the memory of his niece, Mrs. Ingeborg-Marion Lucas-von Busse, he emigrated to Brazil only after 1933 with his wife, who is assumed to have been of Jewish origin. The exhibition catalog mentions, without providing specific dates, that von Busse assumed "a teaching post at the German Olinda School in Sao Paulo" which was "one of his fond memories."

The two editions of the *Erotic Comedy Garden* differ, apart from slight textual variations not only in layout but also in the illustrations. Two painters were involved: Rudolf Pütz (1896–1986) from Berlin and Ludwig Kainer (1885–?) from Munich, who also illustrated Granand's *Lovers' Fairy Tales*. The first private edition, on which this translation is based, contains six drawings by Rudolf Pütz. One hundred numbered copies of this edition were published as a "limited luxury edition," for which "the drawings were hand-colored and signed by the artist," according to

---

7 Erwin Busse-Granand, *Francesco Guardi and the Minor Masters of Venetian Rococo* (Leipzig, 1925).
8 This information is found in the *Genealogical Handbook of German Nobility*.

the publisher's imprint in the unnumbered and less luxuriously designed edition. In contrast, no. 47 of the "Luxury Edition" (on which the republished German edition was based) contains the handwritten note: "The drawings of this copy were colored by the author Granand." Accordingly, there seem to have been two versions of the private edition, colored either by Pütz or Granand.

For the second edition, the title page of which bears the note on the back: "First public edition. 2. to 5. Thousand," Ludwig Kainer, a very popular and prolific painter, set designer and illustrator of books and magazines at the time, provided five watercolor drawings and a book cover designed with green ink.

Most of the images that Pütz and Kainer created for the *Erotic Comedy Garden* show naked young men or young male couples in an embrace, but all of these representations are so discreetly done and modest that they only quite indirectly illustrate the stories which leave little to be desired in terms of frank and full descriptions. It seems quite unlikely that the pictures could have contributed to the prohibition of the book for indecency. The letter to Max Martersteig, in which Granand asks for a statement against the accusation of lewdness confirms this, since in it he expressly only asks for the text to be appraised. In addition, it contains Granand's remark that Pütz's drawings are "artistically very modest, of course." We do not know whether Kainer's illustrations were more in line with Granand's taste.

Although one of the German-speaking world's encyclopedias of artists has an extensive entry that reflects Kainer's status at the time, almost nothing could be determined about his later life and work, and even the date and place of his death are unknown.[9]

---

9   Thieme-Becker, *Allgemeines Lexikon der bildenden Künste* 19 (1926), 440. "During the years 1904–1914 he was attached to the 'Russian Ballet'... He is currently one of the most charming painters of ladies of society and of the night that Germany has at the moment."

The latest evidence of his activities relates to the year 1933: On November 28, 1933, Johann Strauss's *Fledermaus* premiered under Max Reinhardt's direction at the Pigalle Theater in Paris, for which Kainer had designed the set and the costumes. As a set and costume designer, Kainer had worked with Reinhardt several times since 1920; the Paris production of *Fledermaus*, which was no longer performed as planned in Berlin for political reasons, was their last work together.[10]

Another biographical yet inconclusive detail about Kainer was found by chance in the Berlin gay magazine *Die Freundschaft* [Friendship], which in 1925 printed a list of individuals who had signed the well-known petition organized by Hirschfeld against § 175 of Weimar Germany's constitution (criminalizing homosexuality). In addition to such prominent men as the President of the Reichstag (Germany's parliament), Paul Löbe, the composer Franz Schreker and the architect Bruno Taut, Ludwig Kainer's name is also found there (listing New York as his place of residence at the time).

MANFRED HERZER
Berlin

---

10 Huesmann, op.cit.

GRANAND
Life and Works

1885   January 12. Erwin Oskar Leopold von Busse (pseudonym Granand) is born in Magdeburg, Germany, to Lieutenant Hugo Maximilian von Busse (an officer in the Prussian Army) and his wife, Marie Louise Elizabeth Helene (born Weste). As part of a noble family, he uses the title "Ritter" [knight] in his name.

1898   Over several years, attends various military academies.

1905   Graduates from the main Prussian military academy, in Gross-Lichterfelde, outside Berlin.

1907   After two years of military service, begins study of law and art history in Munich.

1909   Abandons pursuit of law degree to study art history.

1912   Interrupts his studies to take part in an expedition to Brazil, followed by a lengthy stay in Paris.

        Continues his studies at the University of Bern.

        Writes an essay about the painter Robert Delaunay for the journal *Der Blaue Reiter* [The Blue Rider].

1914   Earns doctorate in art history from the University of Bern; seems to move directly from there to Berlin.

1917   Appears in Berlin directory as director and dramaturge at the Deutsches Theater, where he works under Max Reinhardt.

            Works as an editor of the theater publication *Die Scene* [The Scene].

1918–19   Directs at least three chamber productions at the Deutsches Theater.

            Directs the world premiere of James Joyce's play *Exiles* in Munich. A copy of his director's notes is held by the Archive of the City of Munich.

1920   Moves to Munich, where he works under Hermine Körner at the Schauspielhaus. Prints a private edition *Erotische Komödien-Gärtlein* [Berlin Garden of Erotic Delights], using the pseudonym "Granand," with drawings by Rudolf Pütz, and a public edition with drawings by Ludwig Kainer (Berlin, Almanach-Verlag). Both are banned by a regional court in Berlin.

1921   Directs at least two plays: George Bernard Shaw's *Candida*, with Hermine Körner in the title role, and *Die Soldaten* [The Soldiers] by Jakob Michael Reinhold Lenz. Both editions of *Erotische Komödien-Gärtlein* are banned by a regional court in Leipzig. As a result of the court decisions, all editions, according to § 41 of the German Criminal Code, are confiscated and "made unusable." The public prosecutor's office seeks but fails to reach a similar ruling against Granand's more harmless and strictly heterosexual *Liebesmärchen* [Lovers'

Fairy Tales], literary imitations of selections from Washington Irving's *Tales of the Alhambra*, published by Almanach-Verlag.

1923 About this time, he ends his work in the theater.

1925 By this time he has added his pseudonym to his real name and calls himself Erwin von Busse-Granand. Publishes an eighteen-page essay on the Venetian painter Francesco Guardi, including a selection of twenty reproductions of Guardi's artworks.

1931 Participates in a group exhibit, *Salão Revolucionário*, in the Escola Nacional de Belas Artes (ENBA) in Rio de Janeiro.

1933 Around this time, converts to Catholicism. Marries in London on April 10 and emigrates to Brazil with his wife, Simonette Mathilde Kowarick, a native of Brazil; according to Granand's niece, she is assumed to be of Jewish origin. The exact date of his departure from Europe for Brazil is not precisely known.

1939 Busse dies in São Paulo on April 10. Gallery owner Theodor Heuberger organizes a commemorative exhibition in Rio de Janeiro, publishing a small catalog containing reproductions of several paintings by Busse, two shorter texts ("Impressions of Brazil"), a directory of his artistic oeuvre, and a brief biography; unmentioned are his two short story collections.

ACKNOWLEDGMENTS

To my entire family and to all my friends, especially the St. Paulites. Love is all you need.

To Mary Bahr and Ulrich Baer, of Warbler Press, who understood immediately the importance of Granand's collection of stories. This book would not exist without their cheerful, unflagging encouragement. They have my deepest gratitude.

To the Schwules Museum and A Different Light bookstore (RIP), each of which can reasonably lay claim to being the place where I first discovered Granand's stories.

To the many health professionals, including friends, who have cared for Marvin: Their efforts have given hope.

To all our tenacious Border Terriers, who each in turn through the years has sat by patiently, waiting for me to complete this project: Ziggy, Daphne, JaJa, Tavo.

And above all, to Marvin Taylor, always my first reader and final critic.